MANUSCRIPT FOR MURDER

MANUSCRIPT FOR MURDER

Roger Keevil

a Ramston murder mystery

also by Roger Keevil

THE INSPECTOR CONSTABLE MURDER MYSTERIES
Murderer's Fête
Murder Unearthed
Death Sails In The Sunset
Murder Comes To Call
Murder Most Frequent
The Odds On Murder
No Bar To Murder
The Murder Cabinet
The Game Of Murder

THE COPPER & CO MURDER MYSTERIES
Honeymooner's Murder
Murder At Witch's Holt
Buccaneer's Murder

THE RAMSTON MURDER MYSTERIES
Murdered By Moonlight

MANUSCRIPT FOR MURDER

by

Roger Keevil

Cover design by Christopher Brooke

mail@rogerkeevil.co.uk
www.rogerkeevil.co.uk

Prologue 1538

The sound of hooves on the cobbled Great Court outside grew ever louder as fresh arrivals crowded in through the gatehouse. Within the incense-fragranced gloom of the abbey church, a tense silence reigned, broken only by the occasional distressed whimper from one of the younger novices. Outside, there was a confusion of shouting and running feet, before a commanding voice succeeded in over-topping the hubbub and bringing it within bounds. Brisk orders were barked, and within moments, armed men had appeared at both the door to the cloisters and the Jerusalem Porch. Their sudden inrush was halted, and a superstitious hush fell on them, as they took in the sight of the group of nuns standing in the chancel before the altar, clustered behind a tall figure clad in dramatic black and white, gazing fearlessly towards the interlopers, a large jewel-studded crucifix held steadily in her out-stretched hand. After a few moments one of the new arrivals, bolder than his fellows, made for the Great West Door and, with some effort, succeeded in drawing back the massive iron bolts and throwing the door open with a resounding crash.

Immediately, a figure on horseback appeared in the lofty doorway, provoking anguished cries from the group of nuns, which were instantly stilled at the stern command from their leader of "Sisters! Calm yourselves!"

The mounted figure slowly advanced along the nave towards the altar, the horse's shoes striking sparks from the flagstones of the floor. At length, as it reached the rood screen, it halted, and stood surveying the women gathered before it.

After several long moments, the leader of the nuns stepped forward, her crucifix upraised in a gesture of defiance. "Sir!" she declared in ringing tones. "You defile

God's house!"

A slow sardonic smile spread across the horseman's face. "God's no longer, I think, madam," he drawled. He drew a document from a pouch at his waist. "But rather, the King's."

Chapter 1
Saturday/Monday

"Thrilling, isn't it?"

"Sorry? What is?" Tania Faye, chief librarian, looked up from her computer screen, where she had been attempting to make sense of an email from the Public Lending Rights organisation about the levels of borrowings from her branch of the county's libraries over the past year.

"The news from the abbey, of course."

"Sorry, Jenny – I'm not with you."

"The discovery. I've been looking up the latest on the news feed." Jenny held her phone out for Tania's inspection. "The mysterious box. It was on last night's news."

Jenny Chandler, a sturdy young woman somewhere in her late thirties, was Tania's part-time volunteer assistant librarian, combining a Saturday shift to help out on Ramston Central Library's busiest day of the week with her regular job as a dental nurse at St George's Surgery on the opposite side of the Market Square. Her enthusiasm was occasionally marred by a somewhat haphazard approach to her duties, and fond of her as Tania was, she was sometimes forced to shake her head in despair as she followed her colleague around the library in order to re-file misplaced books. But now, as Jenny's eyes sparkled with excitement behind her owlish glasses, Tania couldn't help echoing the other's smile as she reached out for the phone.

"We didn't see the news last night," explained the chief librarian. "Ron took me out for an early supper yesterday evening at the Cross Keys, and then we went to the cinema. He wanted to see that new Indiana Jones film."

"Oh, that's perfect!" enthused Jenny. "History and

mystery all mixed up together. Just like now. See, that's what they say in the news story."

Tania bent her head to read the phone screen. "Ramston Abbey in the news?" she smiled. "That doesn't happen very often. What have they done to deserve that?"

*

The Abbey Church of Saint Elfleda had been founded in the hamlet of Hramstune in the eleventh century by an Anglo-Saxon king's niece who became its first abbess. It soon acquired a reputation for fine scholarship, and the abbey's nuns were particularly famous for the creation of exquisitely illuminated holy books, some of which found their way into the royal courts of Europe. And when the founding abbess was made a saint, after her death at the immense and unheard-of age of one hundred and three, her tomb became a destination for pilgrims from far and wide. The abbey prospered, and the early humble buildings gave way over time to far grander structures, with a lofty nave with towering Norman pillars rising high above the modest houses and shops of the small town which grew up around the skirts of the abbey's precincts. But nothing could last for ever, and when Henry VIII's eyes fell upon the wealth of the religious houses in the sixteenth century, Ramston Abbey could not escape the fate of its fellows, and seemed doomed to demolition, were it not for the burghers of Ramston, who loved their church and its saint. A plea went to the king, and for the then enormous sum of three hundred pounds, the town was permitted to buy the main building to serve as its parish church, while other parts of the precinct - cloisters, refectory, chapter house, infirmary - were swept away, leaving only a fragment of the original Saxon foundation in the form of the small side chapel of Saint Elfleda, hastily renamed in honour of Saint George to avert the unwelcome attentions of the king's commissioners. Of the rest, only the former gatehouse remained, becoming an inn on the opposite side of what was now the Market Square.

And now, Tania read, after several hundred years of welcome and untroubled relative obscurity, Ramston Abbey once again found itself attracting attention. During works to repair a piece of crumbling masonry, a discovery had been made which looked set to excite mediaeval historians. A manuscript, some said. As yet, the abbey authorities were trying to remain tight-lipped about the details, but it was clear from the general air of suppressed excitement that there was something significant in the wind. The question on many other lips was, what?

*

Peter Hawkley unlocked the door to the Jerusalem Porch, ready for a fresh week of visitors, before replacing the heavy key in the discreetly-located cupboard concealed in the angle of the adjacent buttress and re-setting the combination. He swung open the heavy studded oak door with only the slightest protesting groan from its ancient cast-iron hinges, and stepped down on to the flagstones of the inner porch, switching the light on as he did so. The slightly musty gloom somewhat diminished, Peter picked up the sandwich board which laid out the hours for tourist visits and services, prior to placing it outside on the gravel path which snaked around the side of the abbey from the Great West Door. As he lifted the sign, he grimaced slightly. Wouldn't it be nice, he thought, if today was one of the days his back didn't play up with one of its ever-more-frequent twinges. He gave a rueful hint of a smile. It was only to be expected. Nobody stayed young for ever. And although his mirror told him that he was seventy-one, and according to so many people, looking pretty decent for his age, he could never quite come to terms with the fact that, inside his head, he was still the same eighteen-year-old who had left the Abbey Grammar School all those years ago, ready to go out and conquer the world.

But, he reflected, it's odd that fate has a habit of bringing us back in a circle to where we began. At university to study chemistry, he had met and fallen in love with a girl from Bristol, and at the end of their courses they had both moved to that city, he to take up a very junior post in the marketing department of one of the larger pharmaceutical companies, and she to become a solicitor's clerk at a minor local law firm. The two married, and continued to pursue comfortable if unspectacular careers, until the day came when Peter's firm was taken over by a massive international conglomerate whose marketing function was run entirely out of their headquarters in Chicago, while at almost exactly the same time, the partners in his wife's law practice took the decision to relocate to London. Neither wanted to follow their employers into such an uncertain future, but at that point, destiny intervened in the form of Peter's father, who decided to retire from his career running a pharmacy in Ramston. Peter, with some trepidation, stepped into his shoes, and found himself operating the family firm for many years, while his wife set up her own small business offering property conveyancing and will drafting. Now a childless widower, and with the pharmacy sold to a national chain, Peter had sought to fill the empty hours since his wife's death by volunteering as a tourist guide at the abbey, returning to the building where he had worshipped as a boy, and had recently become head guide on the retirement of his ancient predecessor.

Peter passed from the porch into the main body of the church, opened a panel, and began to turn on, one by one, the large bank of switches behind it. As he did so, the interior of the abbey sprang gradually into life as the spotlights along the nave, and then the illumination in the side aisles, lit up the simple but stately stonework with its distinctive rounded Romanesque arches, offset by the surprisingly exuberant fan-vaulting of the chancel. Then, as he always did, he set off on a circuit of his domain, enjoying the calm silence of centuries before returning to his counter by the entrance to face the activity of the day ahead.

*

Pandora Weston settled herself at her desk in the study in the attic of her tiny Victorian terraced cottage in the heart of Ramston, switched on her laptop, and then sat back to think for a few moments while it opened up. No point in wondering 'what next?', she mused. It was really pretty obvious. As soon as the proofing of her current novel was finished, which she happily admitted was one of the more tedious tasks in the work of creation, she could turn her attention to thinking how to craft a new story around the bones of the news about the discovery at the abbey. Modern or historic, she wondered? The discovery or the concealment? Already there were thoughts regarding a possible plot line swirling around unbidden in her head, although it was frustrating that so little detail had so far emerged. Doubtless it would in time. Meanwhile, there was this masterpiece to complete. She smiled wearily and clicked the keyboard to open the file at the point in the text she had last reached.

Pandora, somewhat angular and with an untidy shock of crinkly greyish-blonde hair, was something of a local celebrity. At the age of forty-seven, she was the author of some fourteen novels, most of them falling into the modern 'Aga-saga' category, with dashing heroes usually called Henry or Rupert, but with two or three, written under the name of 'Pandora Hope', diverging into the realms of crime and skulduggery during the early Tudor period, featuring Sister Catherine de Grylls, an ancient nun with a nose for trouble.

As the screen blossomed into life in front of her, Pandora reached for her glasses and prepared to continue proof-reading her book. She felt happiest doing the work herself, confident in her ability to spot those irritating typos which seemed to have sprung from nowhere, particularly in view of an early unhappy experience after relying on a proof-reader recommended by her publisher, which led to the first print run of her novel 'Busted Flush' having to be withdrawn, littered as it was with un-spotted errors. Needless to say, that particular proof-reader had not lasted long, and now Pandora preferred to have control over the entire process of writing and editing. With a deep breath, she prepared to settle to her task, only to be interrupted by the ringing of her phone. 'Blast!', she thought. 'I knew I should have left it downstairs.' A glance at the screen showed that it was her publisher calling.

"Antonia. What can I do for you?"

"*Pandora, darling,*" gushed the voice at the other end of the phone. "*It's more a question of what I can do for you. Because I met the big boss of one of the bookshop chains last night at a cocktail party. We got chatting about your books, and guess what?*"

"I can't imagine, Antonia. Do tell."

"*He's up for having you do a series of book-signings in their shops. I told him that your new novel is almost ready, and he knows how well you sell, so he wants you to start off at their flagship store in Oxford Street, and then go on a tour – Leeds, Edinburgh, Manchester – all sorts of places. What do you think of that?*"

"It sounds exhausting, Antonia. But if you think it's a good idea ..."

"Oh, I do, darling. An opportunity not to be missed."

"Well, then, I can see how it could be good for both of us. Let me give it some thought."

"The thing is, darling ..." A note of reserve entered Antonia's voice. *"We're on a bit of a tight schedule. He wants to get things moving the month after next. So I was just wondering ..."*

"Yes?" Pandora felt she knew what was coming.

"How's it going with the current book? You know I hate to pester, darling, but ..."

"Don't flap, Antonia," interrupted Pandora. "I'm almost there. A couple of days and I'll be finished, and then you can swing into action."

"Oh good." The relief was plain to hear in Antonia's voice.

"In fact," continued Pandora, "the sooner I finish, the happier we shall both be. I'm just putting some thoughts together for a new novel, because we've had some local news which I think could make perfect material for another Sister Catherine mystery."

"How exciting, darling. Everyone loves Sister Cat. Well, on that note, I'd better not hold you up any longer. And I'll get on to James with the good news about the signings. I'll be in touch. Toodles!" Click.

With a wry smile, Pandora gazed out of the dormer window in the study, across the slates and tiles of Ramston, to where the roof-line of the abbey was outlined against the sky. 'Yes,' she thought. 'Definitely Sister Catherine. Once I've got this one sorted.' She turned her attention back to her laptop screen.

*

"Tom! I'm just off. Back around eight," Robin Barton, compact and with a flop of dark curling hair that made him look younger than his twenty-eight years, called up the stairs of the modest two-bedroom terraced house a few streets away from Pandora's cottage.

"Sorry?" His husband emerged on to the landing, vigorously towelling his hair. "Didn't catch a word of that."

"I said I'm just off to work," repeated Rob. "And don't forget I've got bell-ringing practice after school, so I won't be home until about eight o'clock."

"No worries," Tom reassured him. "I'm running a spinning class at half-past six, so you'll probably beat me back here anyway. So if you want, you could pick up a takeaway on your way home."

"Okay. Will do. Fish and chips suit you?"

"Great," replied Tom with a grin. "That'll do both our waistlines a power of good."

With an answering laugh, Robin stepped out on to the pavement, closed the front door, and started out on the short walk to the Abbey Grammar School, still determinedly retaining its traditional title despite many changes over the years, passing in and out of local government control with numerous alterations in the law. It finally succeeded in breaking away from the national educational system to establish itself as a fee-paying independent school, which nevertheless managed to offer a significant number of free scholarships to local boys and girls, thanks to several substantial historic endowments, together with many generous bequests from former pupils.

Robin, one of those local boys with a clutch of good exam results to his name, had studied music at one of the minor colleges at the University of Camford, and had then gone on to teach at a grim soulless concrete comprehensive in a city in the Midlands. After an early life in the moderately-paced and friendly atmosphere of Ramston, followed by the gracious surroundings of Camford, Rob came to the conclusion that the big city life was not for him. He tried to build a circle of friends, without a great deal of success, since he found very little in common with his teaching colleagues, but then a marked change came into his life when he joined a local gym. He met Tom Headley. The pair began simply as friends, Tom as one of the instructors, Rob as a sometimes struggling and marginally overweight participant in some of the exercise classes. But what started as an occasional visit to the pub for a drink afterwards developed into something deeper, and the couple moved in together. One night, halfway through the second bottle of wine, the conversation moved unexpectedly on to the topic of the future, and each was faintly surprised to discover that the other was quietly longing to escape from their routine, with Tom growing steadily more resentful of the pressure put on all the staff at his branch of the massive national network of gyms to recruit fresh members and to pack more paying classes into the day. Then, suddenly, a way ahead opened. Rob saw an advertisement in an educational newspaper for a post at the Abbey school, while at the same time, Tom heard from a colleague at work of a new small independent gym being opened by a friend in Ramston. The two pursued enquiries, and in a matter of weeks, Rob had been offered the position of assistant music master at the school, while Tom became one of the three instructors at the new gym at a small industrial estate on the outskirts of the town. They rented a slightly scruffy house in one of the muddle of streets in the heart of Ramston, decorated it in a plain but stylish way, and with a joint sigh, settled down to enjoy life with a different but more agreeable set of challenges.

Rob's route took him along a section of the local river as it snaked its way through the town. He smiled quietly as a memory popped up in his mind.

"Shall we get a dog?" Tom had asked one evening, out of the blue, as the two had strolled along the river bank.

There was a pause. "Actually," said Rob, "I was thinking ..." He took a deep gulp of air and turned to the other. "Maybe ... maybe we could get married?" He lifted his head to look deep into Tom's eyes, which were blinking in momentary surprise, before the two were suddenly hugging, laughing and crying at the same time.

Finally, they broke apart, and Tom wiped his eyes with the back of his hand. "I think," he said unsteadily, "that's a 'yes'."

Chapter 2
Monday

"Morning, Heather!" came the cheery greeting, as Heather Clanville bustled her way into the abbey in her customary slightly flustered way.

"Oh! Hello, Peter," she replied. "Not late, am I?" she enquired anxiously. "Only I got held up by the kids, as usual. Abigail couldn't find her homework, so we had to turn the house upside down to find it. And then it came to light hidden away in the bottom of her backpack after all. And after all that, Ryan found that his bike had a puncture, so the pair of them had to set off at a run. So by the time I had got the washing on the line and then taken the stuff for supper out of the freezer, and then I realised that I was short of pasta and tomatoes, so I had to call into the supermarket on the way here, and now I don't know whether I'm coming or going."

"Don't you worry," soothed Peter in his best avuncular manner. "It's only just gone ten, and there hasn't been a sniff of a visitor as yet, so you've got plenty of time to open up. So why don't you go and do that, and I'll nip into the café and get us both a cup of tea before the onslaught begins?"

"That would be lovely. Thank you, Peter." Heather made her way through to the abbey souvenir shop, carefully located in one of the transepts adjacent to the exit at the end of the recommended visitor route, plonked down her bag of shopping with a sigh, and looked around her tiny kingdom, wondering where to begin.

Heather, comfortably proportioned in a mumsy way, and looking a little more mature than her thirty-eight years warranted, had been running the abbey shop for some five years now. Since the day her commuter husband, an extremely ambitious and very highly-paid executive in a technology company, had chosen the brighter lights of the firm's London head office over her, together with the more obvious charms of his then confidential person assistant, now his trophy wife, Heather had been left to bring up the couple's two children on her own. Fortunately, she had been spared a financial struggle. Her husband, with somewhat belated feelings of guilt, had been very undemanding in the divorce settlement and, eager to turn a fresh page, had ceded her the house, together with a substantial amount of money for the support of herself and her children. Heather, with no need to work, was reduced to a daily regime of shopping, washing, cooking, and cleaning, and with the children both now of an age to fend for themselves without constant supervision, she soon began to feel that she needed something more in her life. Occasional morning coffees with old school-friends did little to fill the void until, one day, one of those friends happened to mention that her mother was about to retire from running the abbey gift shop. The opportunity seemed heaven-sent – Heather had worked as a shop assistant in several retail outlets before her marriage, and she felt sure that her abilities had not rusted away completely. She applied for the job, and was delighted to be appointed. The hours were convenient, the salary modest, but that didn't matter. She felt independent and useful.

Recent days had seen a slightly higher number of visitors than usual, and the shop's stock needed to be replenished. There were the brightly-coloured guide books filled with pictures of the abbey, together with details of its foundation and subsequent rise and fall, and more modest leaflets with a suggested visitor route around the building, pointing out the tombs of notables and the most interesting architectural features. There were cabinets filled with souvenirs of all kinds, ranging from museum-quality reproductions of the royal seals from various charters granted during the abbey's long history, to crucifixes carved from olive wood from the Holy Land, candles in all sizes from the tiniest to huge towers of wax which could stand proudly on a cathedral's high altar, Christmas tree ornaments in the form of angels and stars, and a variety of nativity groups, some naïve, some exquisite, in materials as different as plaster and silver-gilt. And to one side, a bookshelf. Bibles, of course, together with works on the ecclesiastical buildings of England, religious art through the ages, and, surprisingly most popular of all, a series of murder mystery novels set in a mediaeval abbey, where an elderly monk adroitly solved a seemingly unending flow of crimes. The latter publications, which had been made into a highly successful television series, inevitably drew the eye of visiting fans, and were in fact one of the main sources of the shop's income.

Heather busied herself arranging the stock to her satisfaction, stood back with a nod of approval, and opened the till to check on the float, just as Peter arrived with two mugs of tea.

"Very nice," he commented. "Now all we need are some visitors."

*

Descending the stairs of his Georgian house on the old main road into the centre of Ramston, Rudolph Wheatley twitched straight the framed eighteenth-century map of the county which always seemed to manage to misalign itself. Why on earth it should do that, he mused, he could not say. It wasn't as if the house was subject to anything significant in the way of vibration, unlike the bad old days, when all the heavy traffic thundering past had made the entire building shake on its foundations, causing more than one of the original panes in the elegant bow windows of the frontage to develop a disfiguring crack. But now, thanks to the building of the by-pass several blessed years ago, the passing traffic on Westchester Road had dwindled to much more moderate levels, although the frequent deliveries to the town's supermarket by, in Rudolph's view, ridiculously oversized articulated freight lorries, still threatened to snarl the town's roads up on a regular basis. 'Maybe,' thought Rudolph with a smile, 'I've got a small poltergeist. One of the previous inhabitants of the building who disapproves of some of my work.' He dismissed the thought, and turned his attention to the much more important business of adjusting his tie in the hall mirror.

Rudolph was Ramston's other celebrity author, although he would have poured scorn on anyone who used the term. He thought of himself, not without justification, as an academic historian, and it almost seemed as if he had deliberately created himself in the clichéd image of such a person. Tall, over six feet, but with a thin frame and slightly hunched shoulders which gave him the faint air of a predatory vulture, a look bolstered by a bald crown to his head and a prominent and sharp beak of a nose, he gave the impression of being older than his sixty-two years, affecting soft shirts in minute checks, hand-knotted bow ties, tweed jackets with leather elbow patches, and grey cavalry twill trousers above suede shoes. His published works, though few in number, were held in high regard in academic circles. A detailed study of the reign of George III, which ran to three volumes, was considered one of the most definitive accounts of the period, while a racier relation of the doings of Queen Victoria's uncles had almost been short-listed for a literary prize. He was the one responsible for the historical descriptions in the Ramston Abbey guide book. And in a startling departure from his usual dense and scholarly style, he had also produced a series of humorous books for use in schools, where the events of the Roman, Renaissance, and Restoration periods, under the all-embracing title of 'Past Preposterous', regularly received plaudits from teachers who found that their pupils actually enjoyed learning about history and its comic aspects, as well as a modest but gratifyingly regular income.

It was the last set of writings which had brought Rudolph to the attention of the local media, most of whose journalists had at one time or another learned what little they knew of history from Rudolph's books. So whenever an article in the local paper required some historical background, or the regional television company needed a talking head to explain the context of some past event when a minor royal was scheduled to visit to unveil a statue, Rudolph was almost invariably the person they called upon.

And today, it seemed, was one of those days. Just as he was settling into an armchair, preparatory to the daily challenge of tackling the Times crossword, the telephone on the small side table at his elbow rang. He lifted the receiver. "Yes?"

"Mr Wheatley?"

"That is correct. To whom am I speaking?"

"It's Olly Sutton at 'Spotlight Today', Mr Wheatley. I don't know if you remember me. I did the interview with you when they were doing the excavations at the stone circle they discovered up on the Downs."

Rudolph searched his mind. Oh yes. A very personable young man. And extremely polite. "Certainly I remember you, Mr Sutton. And what can I do for you?"

"I don't know if you saw the show last night, sir, but it seems that there has been some sort of historical discovery local to you, at Ramston Abbey. And my producer hoped that we might be able to get your opinion on what it signifies."

"I should be only too delighted, Mr Sutton." 'I'd better find out what on earth he's talking about,' Rudolph thought to himself. 'And quickly. Why has nobody told me about this?' "And when and where were you hoping to do this interview? At your studios? I'd need you to send a car."

"Oh, no need for that, Mr Wheatley. We want to send a camera crew to shoot in Ramston itself. You know, get the abbey in the background as you're speaking, that sort of thing. And of course, there'll be the usual appearance fee."

"Of course." A quiet smile of satisfaction. "If you insist. Although it's always a pleasure to help you media people in your mission to enlighten the general populace. So when will this take place?"

"I've got to get a few ducks in a row, sir, so can I get back to you later?"

"Certainly, dear boy. I shall await your call." Rudolph replaced the receiver and thought rapidly. A visit to the abbey was indicated. And the sooner the better. He laid aside his newspaper, headed out into the hall, and reached for his overcoat.

*

"Yes, my lord. Of course." The Reverend Cassandra Milton, Rector of Ramston Abbey, replaced the telephone receiver with a deep sigh and leaned back in her desk chair in the study of the former abbess's lodging, which had narrowly escaped demolition at the Dissolution by becoming the rectory of the church. She closed her eyes and massaged her temples. It took a repeat of the knock at the door to bring her back to the present. "Yes?"

An elderly woman with bird-like features and sparse grey hair put her head into the room. "I've finished the high altar, rector," she announced. "But I didn't know whether you wanted me to do Saint George's chapel as usual, what with ... well, you know."

"Mmm?" The rector's thoughts seemed elsewhere, and she appeared to make an effort to concentrate. "Oh, yes, Louise. Thank you. And I suppose we ought to have something in the chapel, even though ..." She sighed once more. "Why don't you just do what you think best?"

Louise advanced into the room, a concerned look on her face. "Is there something the matter, rector? Not bad news, I hope."

Cassandra forced a smile. "No, no, Louise. Nothing at all like that. It's just that ... I've just had the bishop on the phone."

"What, our bishop? Westchester?"

"Who else?" came the retort, more sharply than Cassandra intended.

"Oh, him." A grunt. "And what did he want?"

"He wants to send an expert in to look at what we've found."

A snort from Louise. "That didn't take him long. It's only been five minutes since it turned up, and we've already had journalists poking around asking questions. Not that I could tell them anything, of course. And I blame that workman. If he'd just left things with you to take a proper look at, instead of sounding his mouth off over in the Cross Keys about finding some kind of treasure, there wouldn't be all this fuss."

Cassandra gave a rueful nod. "You're probably right, Louise. But we mustn't let it distract us from our normal duties, must we?"

"I suppose not, rector." A sniff. "And I dare say I ought to get on with the flowers. I can take a hint, you know."

A smile. "Nothing of the sort, Louise," said Cassandra. "You do a beautiful job. Everyone says your flower arrangements are the finest they've seen in any church. A credit to the abbey."

"Well, it's kind of you to say so," said Louise, mollified. "And perhaps I'll sort out a little something with red roses for Saint George."

"That sounds lovely."

As the door closed behind her visitor, Cassandra's face resumed its troubled look. 'Of all people, why Tarquin?', she thought.

The Rector of Ramston Abbey, at forty-four the youngest person, and the first female, ever to hold the office, was an attractive woman whose plain black-and-white ecclesiastical garb, with occasional surprising flashes of bright colour in her choice of earrings or bracelet, did not detract from her charm. Once in a while, an exotically-patterned waistcoat made an unanticipated appearance on festive days. She was not tall, but her slim figure and upright carriage made her seem so. Her face, beneath its somewhat masculine short iron-grey hair, could sometimes look solemn and a little forbidding, before transforming into subtle beauty when lit up by an unexpected smile. Her occasional laugh, full-throated and generous, invariably came as a surprise and a delight. Always possessed of a more solemn and spiritual personality than her schoolfellows, it had seemed a natural progression for Cassandra to go on to read theology at St. Bede's College at Camford University, and by the time she left, the proud possessor of a Doctorate of Divinity, the route to a career in the Church of England lay open following the first ordinations of women. She began humbly as a curate in a country parish in the far reaches of Wessex, before moving on to her own parish in one of the less prepossessing areas of Westchester. That was where she caught the bishop's eye. So when the previous male rector of Ramston Abbey dropped dead suddenly during a Women's Institute Bring and Buy Sale, Cassandra was ideally placed for so many reasons, personal and ecclesiastical. Other candidates were interviewed, but with an eye on the politically-correct notions of the time, there was never any real doubt what the bishop's choice would be, and since her appointment, Cassandra had gained a widespread if understated level of popularity in the town.

The rector's brow remained furrowed in thought. What had started out as an uncomplicated and minor repair had grown out of all proportion. It had begun when one of the abbey's team of cleaners, while dusting the stonework in the tiny chapel of Saint George and Saint Elfleda, the foundress having been reinstated as joint dedicatee in the nineteenth century, had noticed that one of the ornamental ceiling bosses seemed to be wobbling. A simple job of re-pointing looked likely to solve the problem. But when a mason from a local building firm came to survey the scene, he pronounced that the entire ceiling could be compromised, and the project was rather more major than anticipated. With a sigh of resignation, Cassandra gave the go-ahead for work to begin, and the interior of the chapel was now a spider's web of scaffolding. Not before time. On the morning of only the second day of work, a crash echoed through the abbey, one of the stone slabs between the ceiling's ribs having fallen to the floor, miraculously missing the solitary workman who was undertaking the repairs. Cassandra was nearby, and she rushed to the scene, to find the dust-covered workman picking something up from the floor.

"Are you all right?" she enquired anxiously.

"Oh, I'm fine, missus," replied the other robustly. "And by the look of it, it hasn't even cracked the slab, so you won't need to be paying extra for a replacement."

"And what's that you've found?" wondered Cassandra, looking curiously at the item in the man's hand.

"This?" He held it out towards her. "Looks like somebody's old sandwich box to me. Have you had somebody in here doing work before?"

Cassandra frowned, puzzled. "Not that I know of. May I see?" She held out her hand, and took possession of the box. Some four inches by six, it looked to be made of some dull grey metal, and she carefully eased open the lid. As the contents came into view, her eyes widened in surprise.

"What's in it then?" asked the workman, craning his neck to see. "Someone's mouldy old crusts, I bet." He laughed.

Cassandra swiftly closed the box before the other had a chance to see the contents. "Oh no, nothing like that," she replied, almost succeeding in keeping a tremor out of her voice. "But I think I'd better take charge of it. And I'll tell you what," she continued, summoning up a slightly shaky smile. "You must have had something of a shock. Why don't you take the rest of the day off, and we'll see you again tomorrow."

"Well, if you're sure," said the man, giving Cassandra a rather quizzical look. He consulted his watch. "In that case, reckon I'll pop over to the Cross Keys for a pie and a pint. They do a banging steak and kidney pud." He gathered up his tools, and was gone in moments.

Cassandra, her heart not quite yet returned to its normal rhythm, watched his departure, before making her way back to her study in the rectory, her prize clutched protectively to her bosom.

Chapter 3
Monday

"Cassandra, you've been keeping secrets from me!"

*

Rudolph, intrigued very nearly to bursting point, had hurried to the abbey with almost indecent haste, provoking more than one indignant 'Well!' as he virtually shouldered pedestrians out of his way as he passed along Westchester Street and emerged on to the Market Square. The abbey rose before him, grey and cliff-like, and he made his way around the west end, past the Great West Door which was only ever opened for the most splendid occasions such as a visit by the monarch or, if he was being particularly honoured, the archbishop of the province. Rudolph followed the path around to the Jerusalem Porch, before passing from the bustle of the streets to the calm of the interior.

"Good morning, sir, and welcome to our abbey," came Peter Hawkley's automatic greeting, before the guide recognised the identity of the visitor. "Ah, hello, Rudolph," he continued with a warm smile. "We haven't had the pleasure of your company for a wee while."

"Oh, no. Well, I've been busy, what with one thing and another. You know how it is ..." replied Rudolph, a little distrait. He looked around. "Do you happen to know where the rector is?"

"Actually, no," said Peter. "She was up around the chancel earlier on, but I don't remember seeing her since, and I've only just come back from the loo, so I'm not totally up-to-date with her movements. She'll be about somewhere, I expect. Were you wanting her for anything in particular?"

"No, no," said Rudolph airily. "Just ... catching up, you know."

"Right." And as Rudolph began to turn away, "And on the subject of that, here's something you'll be pleased about. They've fixed your lift. The chap came the other day. And you'll be glad to know that the visitors appreciate it no end. There's been a lot of interest in your display."

The display referred to was the abbey's own small museum of items of historical and liturgical interest, housed on an upper floor above the Great West Door between the two squat towers flanking it at the abbey's west end. The space, once used to house an organ before the installation of the present instrument in the north transept in the latter part of the nineteenth century, had lain neglected and dusty for years, before the former rector had had the idea of converting it into an exhibition space for some of the abbey's modest treasures. There were silver communion vessels, including one chalice that might even have dated to before the Civil War, although the attribution was hazy at best. Carved wooden altarpieces listed the Commandments in peeling gold writing. Sturdy staves wielded by long-dead church-wardens were ranged alongside mortars and pestles brought to light during an excavation of the abbey's midden. Embroidered copes in faded colours were mounted in a wall display above a monumental semi-circular oaken cope chest which was almost certainly Elizabethan. Headless statuettes of saints spoke of a time of religious turbulence. A bronze font from the late mediaeval period, rescued from a now-demolished church at the far end of the county, was one of the more notable items, its interest only exceeded by a piece of stonework which held pride of place on its own spotlit plinth, under a protective perspex box. The exquisitely-carved ceiling boss from the mortuary chapel of a fifteenth-century Earl of Wessex, its details once hidden behind heavy coats of whitewash, had been rescued from oblivion during a Victorian restoration, and still bore major traces of its beautiful original mediaeval decorative paintwork. And with his expertise in local history, it had been only logical for Rudolph to be nominated as unofficial curator of the display.

The only factor which deterred some visitors, particularly those of advanced years, was the need to negotiate a narrow spiral staircase which rose up through the south tower, reaching the museum level before continuing up towards the bell-ringing chamber on the floor above. A corresponding spiral stair in the north tower directed the visitor back down towards ground level. But a generous benefactor, a wealthy aged parishioner who had marked all the milestones of her life in the abbey, including christening, confirmation, wedding, the marriages of her children, and finally her own funeral, had left a generous bequest to finance the installation of a lift, crammed into a tiny space alongside the south staircase, which enabled the less mobile to visit the museum and enjoy the vista down the length of the abbey's nave, culminating in the glorious rose window above the altar, which she herself had so loved.

Wondering if perhaps the rector had, in view of the mysterious discovery, had reason to visit the museum, Rudolph made his way to the foot of the south tower and, declining to subject his knees to the rigours of the spiral staircase, squeezed himself into the lift, emerging moments later on the upper level. For a moment, at the sound of voices, he thought his quest had succeeded, only to find, to his chagrin, that the noise came from a middle-aged couple in matching anoraks who were poring over a monumental copy of the King James bible, reading aloud and chuckling over the words which sounded so comical when the printed letter 's', which looked so much like an 'f', was pronounced incorrectly. With a grunt, he turned on his heel and returned to the body of the church, where he continued his search, casting an eye into the abbey café and even calling through the door of the adjacent loos, before poking his head through the door of the vestry and eventually ending up, irritated, in the souvenir shop.

"Hello, Rudolph," smiled Heather Clanville, as she placed an abbey guide book into a paper bag and handed it to a departing visitor. "How are you?"

"Well, thank you," replied Rudolph absently. "You haven't seen Cassandra, have you?"

"I have, actually," responded Heather brightly. "She was here only a couple of minutes ago. She wanted a copy of the guide book, for some reason. Although I'd have thought she knows more about the abbey than anyone, being as how she's rector and all. But there it is. I didn't charge her." A laugh.

"So where is she now? I thought she might be in the vestry, but there's no sign of her."

"Oh, she went back to the rectory, I think."

A sigh of impatience. "I should have gone there first. Thank you, Heather." Rudolph marched away, leaving Heather regarding his departing back with mild amusement.

At the rectory he found Cassandra's daily cleaner polishing the brass knocker of the front door.

"Yes, she's inside, Mr Wheatley," the woman replied to Rudolph's enquiry. "She's in her study. I expect she won't mind if you go on in."

Taking advantage of the permission, Rudolph made his way along the tiled and panelled hall and tapped on the door at the end. In response to the brisk 'Come!' from within, he entered, to find the rector seated at her desk.

"Cassandra," he said without preamble, "you've been keeping secrets from me."

*

"Oh, Rudolph, there you are. Thank goodness. I've been trying to call you. I'm really not sure what to do."

Rudolph was surprised. He had never before seen the rector other than calm and collected. But now she seemed unaccountably tense. "What on earth's the matter, Cassandra?" he asked, seating himself as she waved a hand at the chair across the desk.

"It's this." The rector opened the bottom drawer of her desk and produced something wrapped in a soft cloth. She placed it on the desk between the two and unwrapped the item, to reveal the box which the workman had given her.

Rudolph's eyebrows rose. "Oh." He looked quizzically at Cassandra. "Not exactly the startling revelation I was expecting from the build-up. It seems to be an ordinary lead casket. All right, it does have something of a mediaeval air about it, but I can't see that it's anything to get excited about. Is this the surprising discovery that I gather is being talked about?"

"Not the casket, Rudolph. Take a look inside." Cassandra pushed the box across the desk towards her visitor.

Rudolph picked up the casket, eased open the lid, and froze. "Oh my lord," he breathed. "Where did this come from?"

"It was found hidden in the stonework of Saint Elfleda's Chapel. We had somebody in to carry out repairs," explained Cassandra, "and this suddenly materialised. And I just had one quick glance at it, and I couldn't believe what I was seeing. I've had another look since. You don't suppose ...?" The rector left the sentence hanging in the air.

Rudolph reached into the box, removed the contents with slightly trembling fingers, and placed it reverently on the desk in front of him. It was a tiny book, much smaller than a modern paperback, bound in tooled dark leather with a gilt clasp holding it closed. He carefully opened the clasp to reveal the interior, leafing through the delicate pages of what he was certain was vellum, covered in tiny exquisite writing with a scattered profusion of capital letters illuminated in rich reds, greens, blues, and gold. But what held the eye was the illustration on the first page. An intricately detailed portrayal of what appeared to be Ramston Abbey in its first incarnation, with finely-drawn masonry in the simple early Romanesque style beneath a dazzling blue sky dotted with angels with harps and trumpets in their hands. Incongruously, a small black devil perched on the roof. And to one side of the building, totally out of proportion as she was, standing the full height of the structure, stood a woman swathed in the robes and wimple of a nun, her tiny features gazing out at the reader with a look of pride. A hand was extended towards the abbey as if to indicate proprietorship.

"Oh my lord," breathed Rudolph once more. "This is wonderful. You know what it is, of course?"

"I think so," said Cassandra. "Isn't it a Book of Hours?"

"That's exactly what it is. The religious person's essential companion. Prayers, psalms, details of the times of the services to be held throughout the monastic day. And this one ... well, I'm a little shocked."

"Why? Are they so rare?" wondered the rector. "Or valuable?"

"Actually, no," replied the historian. "They're probably the most common type of mediaeval manuscript, although the vast majority were very simple in comparison to this. Even quite ordinary people might own one." Rudolph had unconsciously adopted his lecturer's manner. "Of course, there are some very famous examples. The Duc de Berry's *'Tres Riches Heures'* is probably the most outstanding one that we have.

That's in the Musée Condé in France. It's amazing. Anne Boleyn carried hers to her execution, as I think did Mary Queen of Scots. They tended to disappear after the Reformation. But this ..."

"Yes?" Cassandra leaned forward in expectation.

"And it was found where?"

"In Saint Elfleda's Chapel. Hidden," she added with emphasis. "And look at the picture. You don't suppose that it's meant to be ..."

"The saint herself?" Rudolph shrugged. "I suppose ... when did she die? Eleven hundred and something, wasn't it?"

"That's right."

"And ... hold on a second." Rudolph screwed up his face in an effort of concentration. "If my memory serves me aright, the earliest English Book of Hours we have is from twelve hundred and thirty-something. So if this is from Elfleda's time, it would rewrite the book on religious literary history. But without some sort of proof ..." Studying the picture once again, he suddenly caught his breath. "Cassandra," he said, with a tremor in his voice, "you don't happen to have a magnifying glass about the place, do you?"

"I think there's one somewhere," replied the rector, a puzzled look on her face. "Just let me ..." She rose from her place, opened a large cupboard across the room, and rummaged amongst the contents, eventually producing a large and somewhat dusty magnifying glass. "I knew it must be here. I remember the choirmaster had to confiscate it from one of the choirboys when he found him trying to set one of the hymn-books on fire at choir practice one day. Why, what do you need it for?"

"I'm sure there's some writing here," said Rudolph, taking the glass. "It's just alongside the picture of the nun. If I can manage to decipher it. Mediaeval penmanship and my rusty Latin don't make a perfect combination, I'm afraid. But ..." He squinted closely at the tiny words, before sitting back with an astonished look on his face. "Good heavens."

"Well?" Cassandra could not conceal her impatience.

"As far as I can make out, it says 'Let my book show that I built this'."

"You mean ...?"

"That's what it says. This is Elfleda herself. And this is her own book."

*

At the television studios in Westchester, Oliver Sutton put the phone receiver back on its rest and looked up at the camera operator standing alongside him. "Boss says we're good to go on the Ramston story," he said. "Wants it in the can for tomorrow at the latest. I've just got to line up my interviewees." He reached for a piece of paper among the untidy pile on his desk. "According to the researcher, the person I need to speak to at the abbey is the rector, whatever a rector may be. A chap called Milton, it says here. So ..." He picked up his mobile and dialled. "Oh, hello ... this is Olly Sutton from the 'Spotlight Today' television magazine programme. I wonder if it would be possible for me to speak to the rector. Mr Milton, would that be? ... Oh." Olly pulled an embarrassed face. "Miss Milton, then. Would she be available? ... Oh, that's you is it? Sorry about that." Olly cast a sideways glance at his colleague, who was unsuccessfully trying to keep a straight face. "The thing is ... er ... rector ... my producer wants me to do an item about the discovery which has been made at your abbey, so I wondered if you would be free to do an interview on camera say, tomorrow morning? Tell our viewers all about whatever it is. ... Excellent. Now the thing is, I've also lined up a chat with a local historian, a Mr Wheatley, so I'll need to get in touch with him to try to get you both together ...

Oh, he's there now, is he? That's handy. So I wonder, would it be all right if I came to you around, say, ten-thirty tomorrow ... yes, I'll hold ... well, that's great ... at the Information Desk in the church? Don't worry, I'll find it. Thanks a lot. And sorry about ... you know." With a sigh of relief, Olly closed the call. "Sorted."

*

"That was the television company," said Cassandra.

"I gathered. That was what I was coming to see you about. They've already been on to me. So, there we are then."

"How do you mean?" queried the rector.

"Well, it seems all quite straightforward to me. When this journalist chappie turns up, you tell him the tale of how this little book was found tucked away in Elfleda's chapel, and then I can go on to explain all about this kind of book – that's if the great unwashed care that much, of course. And then, once we've had our fifteen minutes of fame, the manuscript can go where it rightly belongs, up in my museum. It'll make an excellent focal point, and I'll write a little something about it to go alongside. Oh." A sudden thought occurred to Rudolph. "That means I'll have to do a re-write of the section in the abbey guidebook. But perhaps we can just do a slip of paper to insert into it for the time being ..."

"Just a second," interrupted Cassandra. "It isn't quite as simple as that. For a start, there's already a story going about that we've discovered some sort of treasure. The last thing we need is for hordes of treasure-hunters invading the abbey in search of gold and jewels, not to mention the fact that our insurance premiums are already quite high enough, thank you very much."

"Well, in a sense, it is a kind of treasure," replied Rudolph, "but once we've explained everything on the TV, that'll put a stop to anything of that kind. Nobody will make a fuss about a book."

"But we can't explain everything, can we?" said a worried rector. "We don't know how it came to be where it was. We're not even sure exactly what it is."

"Oh, and my assessment isn't good enough, I suppose," remarked Rudolph in offended tones.

"I didn't say that," said Cassandra. "I'm sure you're probably right. But there's a complication."

"Oh? And what's that?"

"I've had the bishop on the phone. He's got wind that there's been a discovery, although he doesn't know what, and so he's sending an expert to assess it." A deep sigh of resignation. "Professor Tarquin Langley from Camford University."

There was a pause. "Ah. Him."

Cassandra's eyebrows rose in enquiry. "You know him? Of course, I suppose you would, both being in the same field, more or less."

"You might say that," responded Rudolph drily. "Let us say that our paths have crossed more than once."

"It sounds as if you've crossed swords as well," deduced Cassandra.

"We haven't always seen eye to eye," admitted the historian. "But when you mentioned his name, you didn't sound over-enthusiastic. And I'm wondering why you called him a complication. Don't tell me you have history with him as well?"

An even longer pause from Cassandra. She coloured slightly. "He was a lecturer when I was a student at Camford. Don't forget that this is over twenty years ago. And he was responsible for conducting tutorials on early church history for the people on my course."

"Tutorials? You mean one-to-one sessions?" Rudolph began to get a sniff of a situation. "Are you telling me that, what with the proximity and all ...?" A silent nod from the rector. "Well, I suppose he may have once had a sort of raffish charm. But a lecturer and a student? Awkward. So do I gather it didn't end well?"

Cassandra's expression gave the answer. "And now I'm not sure I can face him."

"You?" Rudolph laughed dismissively. "You are one of the strongest women I know. Look at what you've become. You're a trail-blazer. So we'll hear no nonsense of that kind. And tomorrow, I shall expect you to put on your snappiest waistcoat and get out there in front of that television camera and show the world what Ramston Abbey stands for. And if Tarquin Langley comes looking for trouble, he'll find he's come to the wrong place."

Chapter 4
Tuesday

"So would you say it was valuable?"

"In cash terms?" Rudolph gave a gentle deprecating chuckle. "Oh dear me, no. Not that sort of value at all. There are many of these little books in existence. Of course, this particular one is precious to us here at Saint Elfleda's own church. And valuable in a scholarly sense. But definitely not worth stealing, if that's what you mean."

"Thank you, Mr Wheatley." There was a short silence. "Well, that's a wrap," announced Olly Sutton, nodding to his camera operator, who started to pack up her kit. "I'm grateful for your time as well, rector," he said, shaking hands with his two interviewees in turn. "And now we'd better head on back to the studios. With a bit of luck, if I can get this edited and in front of my producer double quick, we may even make tonight's programme. So I'll be off. 'Bye!" He disappeared towards the Market Square car park at a trot, the camera operator struggling to keep up, burdened as she was by her equipment.

"So, now what?" wondered Cassandra, as she and Rudolph stood slightly at a loss, faintly bemused at the speed of both the interviews and Olly's departure, outside the Great West Door of the abbey.

"The first thing I need," replied Rudolph, "is a cup of tea. Standing around in a draughty square on a breezy morning is not my favourite way to spend the day. I'm chilled to the bone."

"I did rather wonder," smiled Cassandra, "whether the shivering was caused by the cold or due to nerves in front of the television camera."

"Oh please," retorted her companion. "I've done quite enough interviews in my time not to be intimidated by these children from the media. Anyway, why are we still standing here? Let's adjourn to the Holy Grail for a nice warming cuppa and one of Sharon's famous sticky buns."

The Ramston Abbey café, officially known as the Holy Grail Coffee Shop, was located in a small modern addition to the abbey, tucked in between two of the buttresses of the side wall, and reached through a previously blocked-up, but now re-opened, doorway which had given the nuns access to the now-vanished chapter house. It was run on a voluntary basis by a team of mostly elderly ladies who formed the backbone of Friends of the Abbey, and contributed a small but welcome amount to the general running costs of the church. And there was a friendly, but nevertheless fierce, competition among the ladies as to who would donate the most delicious, and therefore the most popular, of the home-made cakes which occupied the small glass case on the café's counter. The whole enterprise was conducted under the brisk and competent eye of Sharon Burley, a generously-proportioned forty-five-year-old supply teacher whose spiced fruit buns were legendary among regular patrons, much to the chagrin of the other ladies in the organisation. She looked up in slight surprise as her two customers entered.

"Good morning, rector," she smiled. "We don't very often see you in here. And Mr Wheatley," she dimpled. "I can't say the same about you, can I? One of our regulars, is Mr Wheatley," she added in an aside to Cassandra. "I swear he's responsible for half our profits."

"Ridiculous!" laughed Rudolph. "You know I only come in out of the rain."

"Course you do," riposted Sharon. "Now, why don't you take a seat, and I'll bring your order over. Pot of tea and one of my buns as usual, is it?"

"Yes please."

"And how about you, rector? The same?"

"That would be very nice, Sharon. Thank you."

Moments later, a tray was deposited in front of the two, with a murmured "On the house, but don't let on to the other ladies," before Sharon disappeared back behind her counter.

"And now," said Cassandra, placing the lead casket with its contents on the table. "What do you think we should do now?"

"It seems obvious to me," said Rudolph. "We do what I suggested, which is to add it to the display in the museum. After the item on television goes out, there are bound to be plenty of people who want to come and see the book. That's going to increase the number of visitors, which won't do the abbey's income stream any harm at all. Sharon's buns will be reaching a whole new audience." He took a bite, and sighed in pleasure. "And I think there's an ideal spot for our new star item. I think it can take pride of place on that central plinth where we have the roof boss at the moment. The spotlights are already there. It's perfect."

"That's not exactly what I meant," demurred Cassandra. "Although I think your idea is a good one. But what if, once Tarquin's had a chance to pronounce on the book, the bishop decides that it's too important or valuable to be left with us, and takes it away to put in the cathedral's own museum at Westchester?"

"I can't see that he'd be so short-sighted," declared Rudolph. "For a start, Elfleda's our own saint. She scarcely ranks up there among the headliners like Edward the Confessor, even though she was his niece. She's really only of more local interest, although I'm confident she'll bring the punters in. So to speak," he added, at Cassandra's wince at his choice of words. "Sorry – I mean worshippers and visitors. But why would the bishop take away something that would stand the abbey in good stead financially?"

"Because it's worth a lot?" suggested Cassandra.

The historian shook his head. "No. I've already said. These Books of Hours aren't exactly two a penny, but ours isn't going to set the auction world alight, if that's what you're concerned about."

"Good." The rector sat back, relieved. "So how did it get into the ceiling of Saint Elfleda's chapel, do you think?" she wondered.

Rudolph gazed upwards in thought. "Assuming that it did actually belong to the saint herself – and she seems to be telling us in the front page picture that it did in no uncertain terms – then it must have been put in the chapel at the time of her burial. You know, to accompany her through Purgatory on her way to heaven."

"But hidden away in the roof?" Cassandra did not sound convinced.

"You're right," admitted Rudolph. "It doesn't sound plausible at all. Something like that would surely have been on display, especially if it was anticipated that pilgrims would visit the abbey to venerate her. It would have been in a monstrance on the little altar, surely."

"Like those finger bones of holy martyrs or bits of the alleged True Cross, tucked away behind a piece of rock crystal and mounted into a crucifix."

"Exactly. Catholic churches on the continent are full of them. And there's no earthly reason why Ramston Abbey should have been any different."

"Until the Reformation, of course," remarked Cassandra. "It always saddens me to think how many treasures we must have lost when Henry VIII's men came calling and swept them all away."

"Of course! That's it!" Rudolph slammed his hand down on the table, making Cassandra jump in surprise and causing Sharon to look across in enquiry, startled by the sudden loud noise. "Henry VIII's commissioners!"

"What do you mean?"

"Don't you see?" said Rudolph, with mounting excitement. "Picture the scene. All over England, religious houses are being shut down, their treasures confiscated, their inhabitants dispersed. And now the king's men are known to be on their way to Ramston. There's no way the abbey can escape the fate of its fellows. But there's one item that the nuns here value above all others, and one that they aren't going to allow to be stolen or destroyed."

"Elfleda's book."

"Precisely. We shall probably never know the exact truth. But whether it was on the orders of the abbess herself, or whether it was some enterprising nun who thought up the idea, the plan was made to conceal the book in Elfleda's own chapel. The nuns must have had to work fast. They must have stripped the chapel of any relics or references to the saint so as not to attract the attention of the royal commissioners. It would have been ghastly if the tomb was ransacked, as so many were. We know they re-named the chapel for Saint George in order to disguise its identity from those not in the know. And then a hiding-place was contrived up in the ceiling, where surely nobody would think to look, and the book was concealed up there. And there it stayed for centuries."

"Do you really think that's what happened?" breathed Cassandra.

"Find me a more convincing explanation," replied Rudolph, a confident smile on his face. "And if Professor Tarquin bloody Langley can come up with something better, I shall be mightily surprised."

"There's still something else that concerns me."

"And what's that?"

"Suppose Tarquin wants to remove the book for further examination? Or even worse, what if he has instructions from the bishop to hand it over to the diocese?"

"Oh no!" Rudolph was adamant. "This is our discovery, our saint, and if Tarquin wants to lay hold of our book, it'll be over my dead body."

"Well, we shall see," replied the rector, a worried expression returning to her face.

*

"Ron, come and take a look at this," called Tania.

Her husband, halfway into a coat, put his head in through the living-room door. "We'll be late for rehearsal if we don't go sharpish," he objected. "And I don't intend to get in the way of Leah's wrath because of some rubbish on television."

"It'll only take a second," replied Tania. "And just for a change, it isn't rubbish. It's about this discovery at the abbey, so I'm interested."

Tania and Ron Faye were leading lights of R.O.A.D.S., the Ramston Operatic And Dramatic Society, and were in the throes of rehearsal for the group's next production, 'Blithe Spirit', the celebrated comedy by Noel Coward in which Tania was playing the principal part of Madame Arcati, an eccentric medium who communes with the spirits of the dead, while her husband had the prominent rôle of Charles, whose second marriage is being thrown into chaos by the ghost of his first wife. The play was being rehearsed under the stern eye of Leah Sutherland, one of the society's leading directors, who had also been responsible for the group's earlier open-air production of 'A Midsummer Night's Dream' in Cornwall, where the comedy had turned to tragedy after the discovery of a dead body on stage.

The pair settled to watch the item on the local television magazine programme, Ron with frequent glances at his watch. At the end of the item, as Tania seemed about to speak, he leapt to his feet. "Right, love.

We'd better scoot. Got your script?" A nod from Tania. "Good. Switch the box off, and you can tell me what you think in the car."

As the car turned out of the couple's drive and headed towards the dramatic society's little theatre in the heart of Ramston, formerly a small local cinema which had been saved from demolition by the strenuous efforts of the group's members, Tania broke the silence. "I think it's all very fascinating."

"There speaks Madam Librarian," grinned Ron. "I'm not sure I'm that excited about an old book."

"Oh, it's a lot more than that," declared Tania. "If it's what they think it is, then it's a big part of Ramston's history. After all, if it hadn't been for Elfleda, Ramston probably wouldn't be here at all. I imagine it was just a couple of wattle-and-daub hovels when she decided to build an abbey here, and whatever village there was would probably have vanished at the time of the Black Death because everybody died off."

"Cheerful as ever," quipped her husband.

"I can't help it if I'm interested in the history of the place," protested Tania. "And you must admit, if they've found something that was owned by the abbey's founder, that's pretty special."

"If it did actually belong to the old biddy," said Ron. "It didn't sound as if the rector and her sidekick were absolutely certain."

"Oh ye of little faith," retorted his wife. "Anyway, I like the sound of the story, and I'm going to go and take a look for myself."

"What, you're going to go and knock on the rector's door and ask if you can have a butcher's at her latest treasure?" scoffed Ron.

"Don't be daft." His wife gave a good-natured swat in his direction. "I think you were so busy looking at your watch that you missed half the story. They said they were going to give the Book of Hours and its casket pride of place in the abbey's own museum, so that's definitely on my agenda. I can easily pop over from the library during my lunch hour. You can meet me if you're free."

"For a lunch date with my dear wife, always," smiled her husband. "It's one of the benefits of free-lance working from home."

"And you're buying, to make up for your Eeyore-like comments," responded Tania. "You can treat me to one of those lovely paninis they do in the Holy Grail. And if you haven't yet deduced that a librarian is going to be excited by the discovery of a historic book," she added, chuckling, "you're going to make a rotten psychic subject in this play."

"I shall make you eat those words, dear heart," retorted Ron, as he turned into the theatre's car park. "And woe betide you if you forget your lines this evening."

*

Rudolph replaced the perspex box and stood back to survey his handiwork. "There. I don't think that could be better."

The rector nodded in agreement. "You're right. It looks perfect."

"And isn't it beautiful, the way the beams from the spotlights pick out the gold in the illuminated lettering? I'm pleased."

"And so you should be. In fact, I think you've done an excellent job in arranging all our exhibits." Cassandra gave a little sigh. "I very often look at the comments in the visitors' book in the shop, and it's noticeable how many people remark on how interesting they find our little museum. Especially with the lift. It's just a shame that our former star attraction has had to be demoted." She glanced fondly at the painted roof boss which had been relegated to a lesser position, although still prominent, on one of the side displays. "I've always thought it was charming, especially the way the little devil is sticking his tongue out, even as he's being consumed by flames."

"I shall do a little notice to attach to the box as soon as I can, so that visitors can understand exactly what a Book of Hours is," stated Rudolph. "But I want to do a bit of research on the internet first, so as to put it into context. Leave that with me."

"I shall," said Cassandra. "And now I don't know about you, but I have duties to attend to. An abbey doesn't run itself, you know."

As the two made for the exit stairs, there was a sudden burst of jingling music.

"Onward, Christian Soldiers?" smiled Rudolph, eyebrows raised. "Now that's what I call a ringtone."

"Blast!" said the rector, reaching into a pocket and producing a mobile phone. "I normally turn it off whenever I'm actually in the church. I don't like the distraction. I must have forgotten, what with one thing and another." She pressed the answer button. "Hello? ..." Her voice dropped several tones. "Oh. Professor Langley." She grimaced in Rudolph's direction. "Yes, this is the Rector of Ramston Abbey speaking. What can I do for you? ... Yes, I have had a call from the bishop. He told me he would be getting in touch with you ... Well, of course we're perfectly happy to fall in with his request that you come and look at our new exhibit. I wonder, did you happen to see the item on local television last night? ... Oh, that's a pity. So you won't know what we're talking about ... Actually, it's a Book of Hours. Rather an interesting one, in the opinion of the curator of our museum here at the abbey ... Oh, certainly. I'm sure he'll be happy to discuss it with you." A sideways look at Rudolph, with a doubtful quirk of the lips. "So when did you have in mind to visit us? ... Of course ... Tomorrow would be no problem at all. Any idea of time? ... That's perfectly fine. Then I suggest you come to the Rectory, and I shall be able to escort you across ... Very well. I shall see you then." Cassandra disconnected the call. "That was ..."

"I gathered," said Rudolph.

"And it's odd," said Cassandra. "I got the impression that he didn't know who I was. Other than my position, of course. And he didn't see the programme last night, so I suspect he hasn't any idea about you either."

"In which case," remarked Rudolph wryly, " it seems that Tarquin Langley has something of a surprise in store on more than one front."

Chapter 5
Wednesday

Cassandra Milton looked up at the sound of a distant jingling from the bell at the rectory's front door. Moments later, there came a tap at her study door, and her housekeeper looked in to announce "Visitor for you".

The rector gave a muted sigh. "Show him in," she said, and managed to achieve an approximation of a welcoming smile.

Her visitor burst through the door with a flourish. His slightly portly frame and somewhat florid features, beneath which could be detected the remains of youthful good looks, were topped with a thick mane of dark blonde hair which did its best to give the lie to his sixty years. "Rector!" he boomed. "I'm Professor Tarquin Langley. We spoke yesterday. How very nice to meet you!" He advanced into the room, hand outstretched, but then suddenly stopped short, before looking more closely at his host and uttering a hesitant "Oh, surely not. It can't be. ... Cassie?"

"Good morning, Tarquin," replied the rector, her tone reserved.

"Is it really you?" The professor seemed unable to believe the evidence of his own eyes.

"I know it's been a long time," said Cassandra drily, "but I'm sure I haven't changed all that much."

"Oh, but you have," responded Langley. "And when I heard the name 'Milton', I had no idea that the Rector of Ramston Abbey would turn out to be you." He stood back and surveyed Cassandra. "Well, well! Little Cassie Milton. And now, look at you. Where did that beautiful long hair go? And that impish smile that used to pop out at unexpected moments? Not what one would necessarily expect from a staid theology student."

"That was all a quarter of a century ago," retorted

Cassandra, the severity in her voice growing plainer. "And I'm certain we have all changed a great deal since those days. In many ways."

"Oh, I'm not at all sure that I have," said the professor with an arch smile. "I can always find so many ways to enjoy myself. As I'm sure you remember."

"There are some things which are best forgotten," replied the rector with finality. "So I think we are far better off discussing the present rather than the distant past."

"Oh, not so distant," said Langley with a smirk. "But as you wish. And in fact, the distant past is precisely what's on our agenda today, surely? Your little discovery?" The tone was patronising.

"Indeed," said Cassandra, doing her best to stop her hackles from rising. "Shall we go across to the abbey and take a look?"

"By all means."

Entering through the Jerusalem Porch, the rector and her guest were greeted by Peter Hawkley, who rose from behind his counter with his customary warm smile. "Rector! What a pleasure. I didn't expect to see you before evensong today." He looked enquiringly at Cassandra's companion.

"Peter, this is Professor Tarquin Langley," explained Cassandra. "The bishop has sent him to take a look at our newest exhibit in the museum. He'd like to hear his expert opinion." She made every effort to keep any hint of sarcasm out of her remark. She turned to Langley. "Peter here is our chief visitor guide," she added.

"I think we're all fascinated by what's been found," replied Peter enthusiastically. "I know I am. I saw that bit on the television, and Rudolph stopped off on his way in this morning to tell me a little more about it. In fact, I think he may still be up in the museum now."

"Rudolph?" Langley's ears pricked up. "I don't

suppose that would by any remote chance be Rudolph Wheatley, would it?"

"Actually, yes," said Cassandra. "He acts as the curator of our abbey museum. I believe you may know him."

"Oh yes. I know Rudolph." The professor's tone was dismissive.

"Well, we shall head on up," said Cassandra.

"And, professor," put in Peter, "if you'd be interested, I'll gladly give you a personal guided tour when you're free."

"I'm sure that would be delightful," said Langley, not sounding remotely interested. "But in the meantime, Cassie ... Rector, I should say ... shall we continue? I'm sure you don't have all day. And I certainly haven't."

"This way." Cassandra was about to start up the spiral stairs leading to the museum, but she was halted by Langley.

"You have a lift? Oh, let's take that. I never use stairs when there's a lift available. Such a waste of energy."

"Of course," said the rector with a tight smile. The two entered the lift, with Cassandra making a strenuous effort to keep as far away from her companion as possible, and emerged on to the museum level, to find Rudolph Wheatley, his back to them, engrossed in poring over the contents of the perspex box on the central plinth. He turned at the sound of the lift door opening.

There was a pause as the two men gazed at each other. "So," pronounced the professor with a sneer. "This is what passes for scholarship in these parts."

Rudolph gave a curt nod. "Langley. I heard you were coming."

"And now," replied Langley with an expansive but demonstrably false smile, "here I am. Ready to give you the benefit of my knowledge."

"I think you'll find that there's not a great deal to be added to what we already know," said Rudolph. "And perhaps you'd like to verify that by taking a look at the explanatory notice I've just added to our display."

"I think I'll take a look at the piece first, if you don't mind, rector," said Langley. "I never like to rely on second-hand opinions." He moved towards the case and cast an eye over the contents, before lifting away the cover and peering more closely at the book and its casket.

There was a long silence, while Cassandra and Rudolph, on tenterhooks, looked on. At length, the rector could contain herself no longer. "Well?" she said.

The professor pursed his lips. "Difficult to say at a cursory examination," he replied. "Tell me, what exactly do you believe this to be? The bishop was a little vague when we spoke."

"We think it's Saint Elfleda's own Book of Hours from when she was abbess here," said Cassandra. "It was discovered hidden in her own chapel, up among the masonry of the ceiling, during some maintenance works. And the picture and the wording that goes with it make us quite confident."

Tarquin raised an eyebrow. "Confidence can so often be misplaced," he said. "Not everything is what it seems. And not all alleged scholars are fully equipped to give an authoritative opinion on matters they aren't completely familiar with," he added, with a contemptuous sideways glance in the direction of Rudolph. "However ..." He bent to examine the book once more. "Hmmm. Well, the leather of the cover certainly appears to be old. That would be an encouraging start. And the parchment of the pages ... again, there is the appearance of considerable age. So unless this is the work of an extremely talented master of the art, I think we can probably rule out the possibility that it's a modern fake."

"Fake?" spluttered an incredulous Rudolph. "Of course it isn't a fake. The place where it was found probably hasn't been disturbed for centuries."

"Your architectural expertise goes that far, does it?" chuckled Tarquin pityingly. "How nice to know. But you really should listen a little more carefully, my dear chap. I said 'modern fake'."

"I don't understand," said Cassandra.

Langley gave a smug smile. "Oh Cassie ... I beg your pardon ... Reverend Milton, I should say. Could it be that, during our long-ago tutorials together on the subject of church history, you may have not paid attention too closely because your innermost personal thoughts were elsewhere?"

The rector fought to control the blush which rose to her face. "Please speak plainly, Professor Langley," she said as sternly as she could.

"Of course. Now, when the bishop asked me to come here, I did a little research about your abbey, just to give myself a touch of background knowledge. As you know, I had at that time no information as to what it was you were claiming to have found."

"Claiming?" grated Rudolph under his breath.

Langley waved an airy hand and continued. "Now one thing I learned was that the nuns of this abbey acquired a reputation for the production of rather impressive illuminated holy manuscripts."

"Which is exactly what we have here," interrupted a clearly still irritated Rudolph.

"Most of which," said Langley, as if the historian had not spoken, "date from somewhat later than the period of your abbess."

"Saint, I think you mean," said Cassandra.

"Ah! And there we come to it." The professor pounced on the remark. "And in the mediaeval period, saints were, if you like, the main tourist attraction at cathedrals and churches. And abbeys. And the pilgrims loved nothing better than a relic of the appropriate holy person or item at which to direct their devotions. I'm sure I don't need to tell you ... well, I certainly shouldn't need to ... that, throughout the mediaeval period, there was a vigorous trade in relics, both genuine and fake. Genuine and fake," he repeated with emphasis. "So let me offer you a possibility. The nuns here were in fierce competition for the pilgrim trade with such headline personalities as Saint Thomas à Becket or Saint Swithin. What if they had no actual relic of Saint Elfleda to set against these? But they had access to the considerable talents of their sisters who were producing the admittedly beautiful illuminated manuscripts for which the abbey was famous. So how difficult would it be to create a book such as this, display it upon the saint's altar, and claim that it had belonged to Elfleda herself?" Langley stood back, hands on hips, to survey the result of his suggestion.

"But ... but that's ridiculous!" exploded Rudolph. "You have no evidence whatever for such a claim."

"Oh, calm down, dear chap," replied Langley, with a dismissive sneer.

"I agree with Mr Wheatley," said the rector. "That's a calumny!"

"No need to get so hot under the collar, rector," responded the professor. "Clerical collar, I suppose I should say." He gave a little self-congratulatory simper. "But are you in a position to rule out the possibility?"

"Of course not," said Cassandra. "We should need scientific analysis of the book."

"Exactly what I was going to suggest," said Langley in triumphant tones. "So what I will do is take the book into my custody, and then have it tested back at my university. For a start, I can study the wording used and the style of calligraphy in the text. There will be terms and forms of lettering which would be totally anachronistic in a book of the age which you are claiming. And then, of course, there would be scope to confirm the age of the vellum used for the pages. I'm sure my scientific colleagues will have a field day carrying out that piece of research."

"Absolutely not," stated Cassandra. "This book is the property of Ramston Abbey and will not be leaving our possession."

"We'll see what the bishop has to say about that."

"I don't care what the bishop says," retorted the rector with uncharacteristic vehemence. "The book remains here."

"Oh dear, oh dear, we are getting a little excited, aren't we?" said Langley. "So let's not lose our tempers. There are certainly things I can do in the interim ... before the bishop, on my recommendation, makes his decision, that is. Which I believe you would be bound to obey, if my knowledge of canon law is accurate. So I will examine the book further in situ ... that is, of course, with your permission, rector." An ironic bow.

"You may do so," conceded Cassandra reluctantly. "But the book stays with us." She replaced the cover firmly over the exhibit.

A nod of acquiescence. "As you wish. But for my examination, I shall require certain items of equipment which I naturally do not have here. I shall need to bring them from home. Perhaps I can return later today."

"If you must," was the rector's curt reply.

"And in the meantime," said Langley, casting a brief glance over Rudolph's explanatory notice adjacent to the display, "I suggest you remove this ... fairytale ... until you can replace it with some genuine facts. So, I shall be back." He strode towards the lift and stepped inside, disappearing downwards as the rector and her companion gazed at one another, expressions of deep concern on their faces.

*

"Ron, isn't it lovely?" Tania leaned forward to take an even closer look at the Book of Hours within its perspex shield.

"Beautiful," agreed her husband.

"I've seen pictures of things like this in reference books in the library," said Tania, "but I've never seen one in the flesh, so to speak. It's much more beautiful than I'd imagined. And look ... see the features in the picture of the nun. The mouth ... and the eyebrows ..." Tania was clearly enraptured. "How on earth do you think they managed to achieve such tiny details?"

"I'm guessing it was probably in the same way that I think Chinese painters used to do in their works of art," said Ron. "Very small brushes, maybe even with a single hair."

"And nearly a thousand years ago, according to the sign. And working by candlelight." Tania shook her head in admiration. "Those nuns were artists."

"Well, there you are. You've seen it. Your curiosity is satisfied, I hope. So now can we go and get some lunch? I'm rumbling."

"Oh, just a few seconds more," pleaded Tania.

"Okay," said Ron with a good-natured smile. "I suppose I just have to put up with the drawbacks of being married to a bibliophile." He turned away and looked down the length of the nave of the church. "You know," he said, looking back over his shoulder, "it must be ages since I've been up here. I'd forgotten quite how spectacular the view is down towards the rose window when the sun is full on it. Ow!" He came to a sudden halt as he banged his knee on the parapet at the front edge of the museum area.

"Oh, do be careful, Ron," said his wife.

"No harm done," he replied, rubbing his knee and grimacing. "My own fault. I should have been looking where I was going."

"Come on then," said his wife, stepping forward and linking her arm with his. "Let's go down to the café and get you some food. That'll take your mind off the pain."

"Actually," smiled Ron, "I am pretty much in agony. I think one of their famous Brie and cranberry paninis may be required. And I'm probably going to have to have a large slice of one of Sharon's cakes for pudding. Purely for medicinal purposes, of course."

"Of course," twinkled Tania. "And since you're paying, I may be forced to join you. Come on, Hopalong." She plastered an expression of fake concern on to her features. "Now, do you think you have the strength to make it to the lift?"

*

As the couple emerged from the lift, they almost collided with a young man who was hurrying in the direction of the spiral staircase upwards.

"Whoa! Sorry, folks," he said. "Bit of a rush. Oh, hello, Tania," he continued, registering the identity of the pair. "I really ought to look where I'm going. But I needed to go up and grab some of my music from the store cupboard up top, because I'm going to be late for one of my pupils. Her piano lesson's due to start in ..." He looked at his watch. "Gosh! Five minutes."

"Don't let us hold you up then," smiled Tania. "But just before you do vanish, that folio of early baroque music you wanted me to order has just come in to the library. So whenever you want to pop in to collect it ..."

"That's great," said the young man. "Maybe tomorrow when I'm not so pushed for time."

"By the way, I don't think you've met my husband Ron. Ron, this is Adrian Hinton, the abbey organist."

"Nice to meet you," said Adrian, with the briefest handshake. He looked at his watch once more. "Sorry, but I really do have to dash ..." He vanished up the spiral staircase.

Adrian Hinton, another product of the Abbey Grammar School, was something of a local prodigy. His talent for music emerged at an early age, and he became one of the youngest ever to gain a scholarship at the prestigious Capital School of Music in London. A brief career on the concert stage followed, but Adrian found in time that the pressures of performing at the highest level, combined with the constant travelling, did not suit him. He felt stressed. And so, to the regret of many, he turned his back on the career, returning to his roots in Ramston. Now, at the age of thirty-one, he was perfectly content to earn a comfortable living as a tutor of various keyboard instruments, with the local world beating a path to his door, and a long waiting list of applicants to become his pupils. And as his reappearance in his home town happily coincided with a need for a new organist at the abbey, the then occupant of the position growing steadily more haphazard in performance as his age advanced, the rector was only too eager to snap up the celebrated returning musician and, on the retirement of his elderly predecessor, appoint Adrian to the post of chief organist.

"Now," said Ron, as Adrian departed, "how about that lunch? I smell tastiness emanating from the Holy Grail."

"Are you sure you can manage to walk that far, darling?" enquired Tania solicitously, failing to hide a smile.

"Phooey!" retorted Ron robustly, and strode in the direction of the café.

Chapter 6
Wednesday

"Good afternoon ... Professor Langley, isn't it?" Peter Hawkley was his usual affable self as he greeted Tarquin, who had crashed in through the door of the Jerusalem Porch, banging into the venerable timbers as he struggled to manoeuvre the two cases he held. "Can I help you with those at all?"

"A little late, but thank you nevertheless," replied Langley waspishly, as he let the cases fall to the floor.

"The rector mentioned that you'd be back to take a longer look at our newest little treasure with some equipment," said Peter. He regarded the professor's cases. "I hadn't realised you'd be bringing the kitchen sink," he added with a little chuckle.

Langley was not amused. "This case ..." He pointed. "... has the things I need to examine your supposed find. And as for the other overnight case, I've decided that I can't waste my time to-ing and fro-ing between here and Camford in order to carry out the necessary lengthy study which the bishop has insisted upon. So I've decided to put up for the night at the Cross Keys across the square. I'm told it has a reasonable restaurant."

"I'm sure you'll be very comfortable there, professor. And the food in their restaurant is really first class."

"I suppose it depends what you're used to," replied Langley. "I shall judge for myself once I'm checked in. Which I would like to do straight away, but in the interim I need to put my technical equipment somewhere secure. I don't suppose you have anywhere suitable, do you?"

"As it happens, sir, we do," nodded Peter. "There's a huge Victorian safe which was once used to store the abbey records in. Big old books, they were. We've got one on display. Of course, it isn't used now, because everything's been transferred on to digital, so we moved it up to the museum. And that was a job, I can tell you. There was no way it would go up the stairs, so we had to get someone in and hoist it up over the parapet with a block and tackle. Fortunately, the head choirboy's father is a builder, so he did it for us for free. Oh, that was a day, as you can imagine." A chuckle of reminiscence.

Langley was tapping his foot in impatience. "Yes, this is all very fascinating, Mr ... er ... Hawkins, but I don't quite see ..."

"So there's plenty of room in the safe to store your bits and bobs," continued Peter. "I can get hold of a spare key for you. So if you'd like to leave that case with me, I'll see it stowed away upstairs."

"Very well," said Langley with some reluctance. "But please be careful. There are some very delicate items in there."

'Well then, you shouldn't go dropping it on flagstone floors, should you?' thought Peter to himself, but forbore to comment. "I'll just pop it behind my desk here for the moment," he said. "It'll be quite secure here for now. Because before you go, I'd like to make good on my promise to give you that guided tour of the abbey. I don't suppose you've been here before, have you?"

"As it happens, no ..."

"Then you're in for a treat, professor. We're very proud of our history here, so with you being a historian like Mr Wheatley, I'm sure you'll be fascinated."

"Not exactly like Mr Wheatley," replied Tarquin with a curl of the lip. "And I really have no wish to put you to any trouble ..."

"Oh, it's no trouble at all, sir," said Peter, who was plainly not going to take no for an answer. "I absolutely insist." He took Langley's arm. "After all, this job of mine is what gets me out of bed in the mornings since the death of my dear wife. She's outside in the abbey graveyard, you know. I feel I'm blessed, knowing that my work keeps me close to her. And I absolutely adore being a guide, and I love trying to pass on some of my knowledge to our visitors. Especially the children. It's what keeps me going, and I don't know what I'd do otherwise. But here, I'm rambling on, and you don't want to hear about me, do you? So, let's start off in this direction." He virtually manhandled the professor towards one of the side aisles. "Now this monument is particularly interesting. It's in honour of a captain of the Royal North Wessex Fusiliers who distinguished himself during the Napoleonic wars ..." His voice faded as the pair moved further down the aisle.

*

"Just the one night will it be, sir?" enquired Dennis Dean, landlord of the Cross Keys Hotel, as he handed the credit card back across the pub's reception desk.

The Cross Keys was a sturdy stone building across the square from Ramston Abbey, being originally the gatehouse to the abbey precincts. But at the time of the dissolution of the monasteries it had been rescued from the fate of so many of the abbey's buildings when it was snapped up at a bargain price by one of the wealthier merchants of the town, who transformed it into a rather grand residence. The core of the structure still showed its mediaeval origins, although it had undergone many alterations over the years, being at various times a barracks for Cromwellian soldiers during the English civil war, an asylum for Huguenot refugees at the time of the French religious persecutions, and finally, in the eighteenth century, a coaching inn for travellers heading to Westchester and onwards to London. Now it held its head up as the principal hostelry in the heart of

Ramston, hosting occasional auctions in its assembly room and sponsoring the monthly farmers' market which took place in the Market Square on its doorstep. And Dennis the landlord, with his burly frame, slightly old-fashioned greased-back Teddy Boy hairstyle, and friendly manner which nevertheless stood no nonsense, looked as if he could well have been constructed out of the same stone as his building, and was universally popular with his patrons, offering traditional English pub hospitality combined with a range of stylishly antique letting rooms and a restaurant which attracted diners from miles around.

"I sincerely hope it's just one night," replied Tarquin Langley, looking down his nose at his surroundings. "It depends on how long it takes me to settle this business."

"Oh, here on business, are we, sir?" enquired Dennis.

"In a manner of speaking," said Langley. "I have to undertake some research work for the Bishop of Westchester."

"Oh yes?" Dennis's eyebrows rose. "So that would be over at the abbey, would it? Anything to do with that book thing they were talking about on the telly last night, by any chance?"

"As it happens, yes," admitted Langley with some reluctance. "But I'm sure you'll excuse me if I say that I haven't really the time to stand here gossiping about confidential matters. I'd be grateful if you'd show me to my room."

"Of course, Mr Langley."

"That's Professor Langley, if you don't mind."

"Not at all, sir. Professor, I should say." Dennis's smile frayed only slightly at the edges. "Oh, just before I take you up, can I just ask if you'll be wanting dinner this evening? We do have a rather good restaurant, though I says it as shouldn't."

"I suppose I shall have to have something to eat," responded Langley with a sigh. "Having had to miss lunch today with all this to-ing and fro-ing."

"Perhaps I ought to reserve you an early table then, sir. Say, six-thirty?"

"I suppose so."

Dennis made a brief note in the diary in front of him. "Right then, sir. If you'd like to follow me." He started up the impressive oak staircase towards the accommodation corridor.

*

"Oh, professor ! Well, that's good timing, isn't it?" smiled Heather Clanville, as she virtually bumped into Langley as he emerged from the gloom of the Jerusalem Porch on his return to the abbey. "I was just coming to ask Peter if he knew when you'd be back with us, and here you are. Happy coincidence, wouldn't you say?"

Langley regarded her with bafflement. "What? Who are you?" he rasped.

"Oh, I'm sorry, professor," gushed Heather. "Peter never got a chance to introduce us when he was taking you round on your tour, did he? I think it was all a bit of a rush, wasn't it? But now he's told me who you are, and what you've come here to do, so I was hoping, as you're such an expert, from what he tells me, and it sounds as if the bishop thinks so too, which can only be a good thing, can't it ...?" Heather ran momentarily out of breath, and gulped in a fresh supply. "So anyway, I was hoping that I could pick your brains, if it isn't too much trouble, because you know far more about these things than I do, and some good advice never goes amiss, does it ...?" She looked brightly at the professor.

"My good woman, I have absolutely no idea ..." began Langley, but Heather interrupted him.

"I'm so silly." She gave an embarrassed laugh.

"You haven't a clue who I am, have you?" She held out a hand, which Langley just looked at. "I'm Heather Clanville, and I'm in charge of the little shop we have here in the abbey. You know, religious books and souvenirs, that sort of thing, as well as that wonderful guide which Rudolph Wheatley has written."

"And ...?" The professor was still baffled as to why this woman was accosting him.

"Well, you see, professor," Heather twittered on, "I was hoping that you could give me some of your expertise as to what I have in my shop and what I ought to be adding. Because you know, it's only small, but we do generate a modest amount of money which goes towards the upkeep of the abbey, and you know what they say, every little helps, doesn't it? So I was thinking, especially now that we have this wonderful new book in the museum, which I popped up to see a little while ago, and isn't it beautiful, so I thought perhaps that opens up a whole new possibility for stock in my shop, and maybe we ought to investigate the feasibility of getting some replicas which we could sell, because I know these things can be quite expensive, but I wondered if you might have some contacts as to where we might acquire such things." Heather regarded Langley with hopeful eyes. "So could you spare just a tiny minute to come and take a look. Please!"

Langley stifled a sigh. It was plain that this woman was not going to let him escape, so probably the best way to dispose of the irritation was to go along with her, look at her little shop, offer a few words of wisdom, and then get on with his work. He managed to achieve a smile. "Of course, Mrs ... er ... Clandon. I'm sure my knowledge of these historical matters is probably much better than most other people's." A curl of the lip. "So ... where is this shop of yours?"

"It's down here in the transept," babbled Heather

happily, as she bustled down the centre of the nave with her unwilling companion in tow. "I'm surprised you didn't notice it earlier on when Peter was giving you your tour, but I suppose you had so many things to take in, because the history of the abbey is absolutely wonderful, and Peter has it all at his fingertips, so I expect you'll have been completely engrossed by what he was saying. I know most of our visitors are, from what they tell me when they visit my shop. That's why so many of them want to take away a little memento, of course." A momentary pause to catch her breath, and then Heather flung out an arm in a gesture of pride. "Well, here we are."

Langley stepped gingerly in through the entrance to the shop, fashioned from a re-purposed section of altar screen which had been deemed no longer appropriate for modern fashions of worship, and looked around him. He took in the tinsel Christmas tree display, hung with its array of glass and plaster ornaments. He browsed the glass cabinets with their whimsical nativity groups and candles adorned with glass gems. His eye passed over the rack of teddy bears dressed in nuns' habits. And his gaze lingered longest on the shelves of books, apparently searching for something in particular.

"Hmmm," he observed at length. "I see you don't stock any of my histories of the mediaeval church. I should have thought that they would be essential reading matter in a place like this."

"Sorry, no," apologised Heather. "I'm not really sure that our visitors are up to reading anything by an actual professor. I'm afraid they might find it a bit ..." She hesitated.

"A bit ...?" enquired Langley, nostrils flared.

"Well, you know, a bit difficult to follow," said Heather. "All a bit too intellectual for the likes of me." She gave an embarrassed giggle. "But they really go for

Rudolph's guide," she hurried on. "That's much more their style. And then there are the bibles. We sell lots of those. The New English Bible's the most popular."

"No doubt," grunted Langley under his breath. "And I see you stock other fiction."

"Other fiction?" frowned Heather, puzzled.

"Apart from Mr Wheatley's guide book."

"Oh, you mean the whodunnits. Oh yes. Ever since that television series, lots of people like to buy those because they can visualise what that monk detective's abbey must have been like. And I've even got a couple by our own local author."

"Local author?" queried the professor.

"Yes. Pandora Weston. Well, Hope, in this case. She's written a couple of books about a mediaeval nun who solves mysteries. I've got some copies there at the end. And apparently Miss Weston says that she was inspired by our very own sisters."

"I believe I may have heard of her," said Langley in condescending tones. "Not, by all accounts, work of very great merit."

"So, professor," said Heather expectantly, "what do you think of my little shop?"

"I'm not at all sure where to begin," replied Langley. And at the sound of muffled chimes from the abbey's clock, he looked at his watch. "Heavens," he said, with an exaggerated start. "I hadn't realised how the time was passing. I really must get on."

"But what about our chat?" protested Heather.

"Another time, perhaps," said Langley, and made his escape.

*

Stepping out of the lift at the museum level, the professor came face to face with Robin Barton who was clattering down the spiral stairs from the bell-ringing chamber on the floor above.

"Sorry, sir," said Robin. "Didn't mean to startle you."

Langley looked the young man up and down. There was a mixture of admiration and speculation in his eye. "No harm done, dear boy," he replied. "Now ... haven't I already seen you somewhere today?"

"I ... I don't think so," said Robin. "And I can't think where that would have been. I've been teaching all morning. I'm at the Abbey School. And then I popped out to grab a bite of late lunch with a friend, and I ought to be back at school now, but I'm taking advantage of a free period to collected the new programme of rehearsals and events from upstairs. I'm one of the bell-ringers."

"Ah, I see." Langley sidled a touch closer to Robin. "A very athletic pastime, I'm sure. Excellent for developing the arm muscles, I imagine."

"Er, yes ... I suppose so." Robin seemed uncertain how to react. His eyes flicked from side to side. "And I've realised who you are. Peter Hawkley told me there was a professor from Camford who's come to look at the rector's newest exhibit here in the museum. That must be you."

"It is indeed. Tarquin Langley, at your service." The professor extended a limp hand, which Robin felt obliged to shake. "Aha!" A snap of the fingers. "And now I've just remembered where it was I saw you. It was out in the Market Square. You were with a rather pleasant-looking young man, if I remember correctly."

"Yes," said Robin briefly. "A friend."

"The friend you'd just had lunch with, I assume," smirked Langley. "Although I'm sure he looked like more than just a friend to me. That looked like a very affectionate peck on the lips that he gave you as you parted." He placed a hand on Robin's arm.

Robin stepped as far back as the tiny landing would permit. "I think I'd better get back to school now, professor," he said hastily. "Nice to have met you." A nod, and he was gone.

The professor, a quiet smile on his lips, made his way over to the museum's central display and leant forward for a closer look at the Book of Hours in its spotlit setting. Stepping back, he looked around and spotted the large safe in which Peter Hawkley had promised to store his case of equipment. He tried the handle, without success, and then, with a tut of impatience, headed back towards the lift to go in search of the promised key.

Chapter 7
Wednesday

Tarquin Langley turned around in slight surprise as the door to the lift squeaked open, to see Sharon Burley emerging, a tray in her hands.

"I've brought you some refreshments, professor," smiled the café manager, setting the tray down on top of one of the side display cases, where faded abbey charters rested under protective glass. "I thought you might need something to keep you warm. This building isn't the cosiest place on earth."

Langley was taken slightly aback at the gesture. "Oh ... I wasn't expecting ... thank you, Mrs ..."

"Burley. Sharon Burley. And it's 'Miss'. Not that that matters. I run our little café here at the abbey. The Holy Grail, it's called. Just our little joke, because we're a little bit tucked away, and visitors are always searching for us. It's not much, but it keeps me going, Well, me and the other ladies who cover for me when I'm working. I teach, you see. Supply, that is, not full-time. But whenever one of the teachers over at the Abbey School is off for some reason, they know they can always get me in at short notice because I'm nice and handy. I always enjoy popping over to the school. The staff are such a lovely friendly bunch, and not stuck-up at all."

"Well, isn't that nice to know?" said Langley insincerely. "In fact, I believe I met one of those teachers earlier on. A young man by the name of Barton, if I remember rightly."

Sharon's face brightened. "Oh yes. That'll be Robin Barton. He pops into my café sometimes with his other half. He's one of our bell-ringers here. Lovely boy."

"Yes, I thought so too," said Langley, a half-smile on his face. "I've always appreciated the art of campanology."

"Anyway, here I am distracting you, and I'm sure you're very busy," said Sharon. "So, I've brought you a hot drink. I didn't know whether you'd prefer tea or coffee, but everyone likes a nice cup of tea in the afternoon, don't they, so I've made you a lovely pot of Earl Grey. And there's a couple of my special sticky buns to go with it. They're always popular with my customers, so I hope you've got a sweet tooth."

Langley winced inwardly. "Well, as you say, Miss ... er ... Barley, I do have work to do, so if you'll excuse me ..."

"Of course," said Sharon. "Sorry to interrupt. I'll leave you to get on." She backed into the lift as the professor, with a contemptuous look in the direction of the tray, turned back to resume his scrutiny of the Book of Hours.

*

"I'm assuming I may keep hold of this safe key," said Tarquin Langley as he approached Peter Hawkley's desk by the Jerusalem Porch.

"Of course, if you wish, professor," replied Peter courteously. "I shan't have need of it tonight, and I have the master key on my bunch anyway. So does this mean you've finished for the evening?"

"Not at all," said Langley. "But I'm afraid that breathing the musty air of this building for this length of time has left me wanting a bath, and in any event, I have a table reservation for an early supper at the hotel."

Peter nodded in the direction of the tray Langley was carrying, apparently untouched save for one bite out of one of the buns. "Well, I do hope that Sharon's little teatime offering hasn't spoilt your appetite," he smiled.

The professor did not return the smile. "Little chance of that, Mr Hawker. I was never going to be tempted by a pot of dishwater and some unpleasant concoction of sugar and fat. But in any event, I intend to return later. I presume I can gain access to your ... I suppose we have to call it 'museum'."

"Of course, professor. We don't lock up the abbey for the night until half past nine. Because what with evensong, and then the bell-ringers very often have a practice session, and likewise the choir, although they don't have a rehearsal tonight, although sometimes the organist comes in if we've got a wedding coming up, and of course there are visitors who can't necessarily get here during the day, and there's always somebody who wants to pop in for private prayers, so all in all, we like to keep open house."

"What busy little lives you lead," remarked Langley. "Now, can you tell me where I can dispose of this tray?"

"Ah, you'll be wanting the Holy Grail, sir. And so many people have told me, it's a devil to find." Peter chuckled at his own joke. Langley did not join in. "I've been meaning to get a better sign. But if you go down that way, and there's a door to the side, and it's through there. I can show you if you like."

"I'm sure I'm quite capable of following simple directions," replied the professor.

"And I'd love to know your thoughts on our little tour of earlier on. I'm sure you can make some suggestions as to how I might improve on it."

"You'd like my thoughts? Then I'll gladly tell you what I think," said Langley.

"Then I'll come with you to the café," said Peter. "That'll save you getting lost." He gave a friendly smile as the two set out in the indicated direction.

*

"Good evening, Miss Weston," beamed Dennis Dean, as the novelist entered the restaurant of the Cross Keys. "That's nicely timed. I'm just opening. Table for one, is it?"

"Yes please," said Pandora, unwinding herself from the voluminous cape-cum-scarf which she usually affected. "I know it's terribly lazy of me, but I just couldn't be bothered to cook this evening. I'm up to my ears with the proof-reading of my new book, which my publisher is badgering me for, and to complicate matters, I've got all sorts of ideas swirling around in my brain about a plot line for the next new novel, which I'm desperately trying to push aside, but with very little success, I'm afraid." She smiled ruefully. "So I thought that the one thing which would take my mind off everything would be to come here and be diverted by some of your chef's wonderful cooking."

"You're very kind," responded Dennis. "We'll do our best not to disappoint you."

"You never do," said the novelist, already beginning to feel a little more relaxed.

"So just let me take that cape for you," continued Dennis, "and I'll show you through to your table – I've got that little corner booth free, and I know you like to sit there - and then I'll bring you the menu. We've got some rather nice specials this evening, including a venison casserole which the chef is particularly pleased with," he said, as he led the way across the restaurant. "And he's not wrong either – I had a little taste of it earlier, and it's spot on."

"In that case, you needn't bother with the menu. I'll happily go by your recommendation."

"And maybe a large glass of your favourite Chilean Malbec to go with it?" twinkled the landlord.

"You know me so well," chuckled Pandora, as she seated herself on the proffered chair.

"Be right with you," said Dennis, and disappeared towards the bar.

Two courses later, Pandora looked up as Dennis approached her table once again. "Here's your coffee, miss," he said, depositing a cup and a cafetière in front of her. "So, if you don't mind me asking, and if it's not a terribly big secret, I'd love to know what this next new novel is all about."

"Oh, it's just a few initial thoughts at the moment, Dennis," replied Pandora as she sipped. "But I'm wondering whether I might be able to use this discovery they've made over at the abbey as the basis for a new Sister Catherine mystery. But don't quote me."

"Well, I'll look forward to that. I always enjoy your Sister Cat books."

"But I've got a lot of work to do before I set pen to paper. Or in my case, fingers to keyboard. I'm sure there's going to be plenty of research needed."

"Oh well then, you couldn't be in a better place, miss." Dennis stepped aside and gestured to the man who had just taken his place at an adjacent table. "Because as luck would have it, here you've got Professor Langley, who just happens to be here on that very subject. Apparently the Bishop of Westchester is very interested in this book thing they've found, and he's got the professor here in to look into the matter. Isn't that right, professor?"

Tarquin Langley looked up reluctantly. "What's that you say?"

"I was just telling Miss Weston about the reason you're staying with us," explained Dennis. "She's very interested in the subject, being an author and all."

"Oh yes?" responded the professor languidly.

"Surely you've heard of her," insisted Dennis. "Pandora Weston. She's a novelist. Writes a lot of those horsey things the women like to read. Specially my missus. Now me, I prefer her other books, the Pandora Hope ones with the mediaeval murders. I expect you've come across them, being a historian yourself."

Tarquin shook his head. "I doubt it. Most

historical fiction tends to be utter garbage."

"Oh, I'm sure you couldn't say that about the Sister Cat books, professor," protested Dennis.

Tarquin raised an eyebrow as he regarded Pandora. "I suppose it's possible I may have seen some reviews. So you're responsible for those, are you?"

"For my sins, yes," smiled Pandora. "So any advice you could give me about the current business would be much appreciated."

"The only advice I can give, dear lady, is to stay away from subjects of which you evidently have no knowledge," returned Langley waspishly.

Pandora drew herself up. Her nostrils flared. "I see. Well, I have no wish to intrude, so I will leave you to your dinner," she said, tight-lipped. "Thank you, Dennis, for a delightful meal. Please tell chef that the venison was a triumph." She stood. "But now I shall be on my way. I'm sure the abbey will still be open to visitors, so I intend to pop over and take a look at this newly-discovered book for myself. I can see that I shall have to carry out my own research, in the absence of any help from anyone else." She cast a withering glance in the direction of Langley, before sweeping out of the restaurant.

*

"Back again so soon, rector?" said a surprised Louise Froyle, turning round from adjusting one of the altar flower displays. "It's not been five minutes since you left after evensong."

Louise, a delicate-looking woman with sparse grey hair and watery grey eyes, and looking every one of her eighty-three years, had been arranging flowers at Ramston Abbey for longer than anyone could remember. Since the day of her confirmation at the abbey by a former and now long-dead Bishop of Westchester, Louise had always thought of the building as her home, and had always done everything in her power to make it a credit to the town and to enhance its beauty. She had begun in a small childish way, contributing simple little bunches of country flowers at the time of Harvest Festival, and as her abilities grew – 'blossomed', had quipped one former rector – she had become a stalwart of the team of mostly women who provided and maintained the flower arrangements on the various altars around the building. Now, and not by reason of seniority alone, she was head of the current team, ensuring that the floral offerings were appropriate to the season and of the highest quality. Despite her age and apparent fragility, nothing escaped her eye, or her still-sharp ears. And as one of the most assiduous worshippers at the abbey, never missing a service, she was a constant presence, always to be seen somewhere within the precincts.

Cassandra Milton smiled. "I might say the same about you, Louise," she replied. "I'm sure if I asked some people, they would tell me that they suspect you sleep here."

"Now that would just be daft talk," said Louise, dismissing the remark gruffly. "Anyway, is there something I can help you with?"

"Actually, eventually, yes," said the rector. "I'm back because I have a meeting in the vestry with an engaged couple to talk about their wedding arrangements. So in due course, I'm sure they'll be wanting to liaise with you and your team about the flowers for the day of the service. But that's for another day. You don't need to wait around to speak to them if you have somewhere else to be."

"Now there's more daft talk, if I'm allowed to say so, rector," responded Louise with a wheezy chuckle. "I always go round last thing to make sure my flowers have got water and strip off any dead petals. What, go back home to my little flat and watch all the rubbish they have on television these days? Not me! Good job I don't have to pay for the licence at my age. There's never anything worth seeing. It's all repeats. Oh, except for that thing they had on the local about our new little book. And I nearly missed that, because I'd had the news on, and I was just coming out after tea to come to evensong, and then I heard them mention the abbey, so I stopped. And I went up to the museum earlier on and had a little peep. Never seen anything so beautiful, I haven't."

"I couldn't agree with you more, Louise. And we're going to make sure it stays here where it belongs."

"Why?" Louise looked troubled. "Do you mean to say there's some chance they're going to take it away from us? Is that what that professor chap Peter told me about is up to?"

"Never fear, Louise," said Cassandra confidently. "That little book is staying with us if I've got anything to do with it."

At that point, there came the loud sound of a heavy door opening and closing, and a young couple emerged hand-in-hand from the gloom of the Jerusalem Porch. "Excuse me," said the young woman shyly. "We're looking for the Reverend Milton."

"And you've found her," said Cassandra, advancing to meet them with a welcoming smile. "And you'll be Sasha and Mark, I expect." Nods. "Do come on through." She led the way into the vestry, and the door closed behind them.

*

The sound of hand-bells in the chamber above the museum eventually fell silent, and a few moments later the sound of footsteps on the stairs and a babble of chatter signalled the departure of the group of bell-ringers at the end of their rehearsal session.

'Thank goodness for a blessed moment of peace,' thought an irritated Tarquin Langley as he bent once more to his examination of the Book of Hours. But only a minute or two later, fresh steps could be heard climbing the stairs, and Langley turned, prepared to be annoyed by the further interruption, only for his sour expression to turn to a smile of delight as he realised that the new arrival was none other than Robin Barton. "Well, well, Mr Barton. This is an unexpected pleasure. I didn't anticipate seeing you again quite so soon." He advanced towards Robin.

"I forgot something," said Robin quickly. "I left a folder with some lesson notes upstairs." Before Langley could reach him, he had vanished up the spiral staircase at speed, returning a few seconds afterwards, a file clutched in his hand, to find the professor standing on the tiny landing and blocking his way.

"Oh, why the hurry, Robin?" said Langley. "I'm sure we can both spare a moment for a little chat." He placed a hand on Robin's shoulder, which the young man attempted unsuccessfully to shake off.

It was two minutes later that a grim-faced Robin strode past Heather Clanville as she headed for the stairs to the museum, and the Jerusalem Porch door crashed closed behind him.

"Professor," said Heather timidly as she entered the museum. "I wasn't sure if you would still be here. I wondered if you could spare a minute."

Langley sighed. "Am I never to be allowed to get on?" he declaimed dramatically. "Very well, Mrs Clanfield. What is it you want now?"

"I was just hoping that we could carry on our conversation about my shop," hesitated Heather. "You see, I was just going through my stock because I'm putting in an order tomorrow morning, and I wanted to know if you could give me any helpful advice as to what I should or shouldn't be ordering. I don't want to waste the abbey's money, after all."

"No," replied Langley. "None of us wants to waste

money, do we? Or time, for that matter. So, you're after my considered opinion regarding your shop, are you?"

"If it's not too much trouble."

"Oh, no, dear lady, no trouble at all," said the professor, with a smile and in a tone that dripped sarcasm. "Well, madam, if you want my frank assessment, here it is."

Shortly afterwards, Sharon Burley emerged into the main body of the abbey, a mug in her hand, to see Heather hurrying down the nave, a handkerchief clutched in her hand. "Everything all right, Heather?" she enquired.

"Yes," came the reply in a shaky voice. "I'm just finishing doing my stock order."

"Oh, right. I was just about to take this tea up to Adrian. He's been practising up in that organ loft for hours," said Sharon, as Heather disappeared into the sanctuary of her shop.

Rudolph Wheatley sat in the calm gloom of one of the abbey's small side chapels and pondered. What, he wondered, was going to be the result of the present situation? Surely, in the excitement of the find in Saint Elfleda's chapel, nobody could have anticipated the kind of upheaval which looked as if it might be looming. This ought to be a happy time for the rector and all her congregation, but instead she seemed pre-occupied with uncertainty. Why on earth, he thought, hadn't the bishop sent anyone but Tarquin Langley to assess the new find? Personal history aside – and there seemed to be an excess of that – surely the abbey ought to be allowed to conduct its own affairs without interference from outside. He sighed. The question was, was anyone capable of stopping the disruption?

*

The scream, when it came, echoed around the cavernous spaces of Ramston Abbey, and was loud enough to bring people running. Cassandra Milton emerged from the direction of the vestry, while Heather Clanville came stumbling from the region of the abbey shop, with Rudolph Wheatley and Peter Hawkley arriving from different areas of the dimly-lit side aisles. The whole group converged beneath the towers at the west end of the church, to find Louise Froyle standing, aghast and shaking, over the crumpled form of Tarquin Langley, which lay on the unforgiving flagstones beneath the overhanging museum parapet, the Book of Hours next to his out-flung hand, a spreading pool of blood surrounding his head.

Chapter 8
Thursday

"Awful, isn't it?"

Tania Faye had scarcely had time to settle herself behind her desk after unlocking the doors to the library when Jenny Chandler burst through in an agitated state.

"Sorry, what is?" asked a startled Tania.

"The news from the abbey, of course," replied Jenny, eyes wide with excitement. "It was on breakfast TV."

'I'm getting a ghastly sense of déjà vu,' thought Tania to herself. "What is it we're talking about?" she enquired. "I missed the local TV news this morning."

"It's all about that book they found over there," explained the dental nurse.

"Ron and I went across to take a look at it yesterday. It's beautiful. Don't tell me something dreadful has happened to it."

"No, not the book. But apparently the Bishop of Westchester had sent some expert to have a look at it, and he's now been found dead! And there's a police car parked outside the abbey. What do you think of that?" concluded Jenny triumphantly.

"Does that mean they think there's something suspicious about the death?"

"Well," said Jenny, rounding the reception desk and settling herself alongside Tania. She looked around the library, to see that Tania's other assistant was occupied re-shelving books some distance away, and dropped her voice to a confidential murmur. "You know me. I'm not one to pass on gossip. But I heard from Mary, you know, the woman who runs the newsagent's shop just over the Square, that it all happened just before the abbey closed last night. She lives in the flat over the shop, and she was sat watching television when she noticed blue flashing lights through her curtains, so she looked out and saw an ambulance turn up, followed by a police car, and not long after that, there was a white van with a couple of women in those white overalls they wear. And then later the ambulance took away somebody on a stretcher, all covered up, so it was obvious they were dead. And Mary heard from her brother, who's a porter at A and E, that it was this expert chap who'd been brought in dead."

"Do they know what happened?" enquired Tania.

"The porter overheard somebody mention 'cranial trauma', but he doesn't really know any more than that. But what I'm thinking is," said Jenny, leaning closer and lowering her voice even more, "if it's all above board, or even if it's an accident, what's that police car doing there?"

"Good point," mused Tania reflectively.

"And that's all I know," said Jenny, rising. She looked at the clock above the desk. "Oh lord! I'd better get back. I only popped across from the surgery because I had a couple of minutes free because we had a cancellation. Alison will have my skin! But I thought you'd want to hear the latest. You being good at finding out all about what's gone on when there's a suspicious death, after that business in Cornwall. I'll let you know if I hear any more." She fled.

After a few moments reflection, Tania fished her mobile out of her bag and dialled.

"Faye Management Consultants, Ron Faye speaking. How can I help you?'

"Sorry, darling, not business, only me," said Tania.

"No need to apologise, love. Far better you than some dull businessman who's got himself into a commercial hole. What's up? Forgotten to take something out of the freezer?"

"No, nothing of the kind," replied Tania, keeping a

weather eye out for her colleague, still occupied at the far end of the library. "But I wondered if you can tear yourself away from work and meet me for lunch today?"

"Two lunches out in two days? And another invitation to dally with my lovely wife?" Tania could hear the grin in Ron's voice. *"If I didn't know better, I'd suspect that something was going on."*

"Maybe it is," said Tania. "Have you seen the news this morning?"

"Not a dickey-bird. I've been heads-down in a load of spreadsheets. What's going on?"

"Tell you what I know over lunch. We might saunter over to the Holy Grail again. Pick me up at one?"

"Very mysterious! Okay, it's a date. See you then."

Tania disconnected, just as her young colleague returned to the reception desk. "Emma," she said, "are you okay to take your lunch break at twelve? I have to meet Ron."

Emma shrugged. "No problem. It's only sandwiches anyway. I can hide myself away in a corner and catch up on my reading. I'm just starting Book Three of a fantasy saga, and I want to find out what the elves are up to."

'No accounting for taste,' thought Tania. "Great," she smiled. "I'll make sure the goblins don't disturb you."

At one o'clock on the dot, Ron Faye sauntered through the library door, just as his wife was putting on her coat. "Ready, love?"

"Perfect timing," said Tania, and the couple made their way out of the library and on to the Market Square.

"So, I'm intrigued. What's afoot?" wondered Ron.

"They've had a dead body at the abbey," announced Tania.

"Well, that's not news," laughed Ron. "The place is stuffed with them. About a thousand years' worth."

"Idiot!" said Tania. "This one's rather fresher than

the rest. In fact, it's only from last night. I gather from my part-timer Jenny, who couldn't wait to rush in to me with the news this morning, that it's this history professor they've got in from Camford University to look at the new book."

"So? This chap might just have dropped dead for any number of reasons. What's got you so interested?"

"Ambulance in the middle of the night? Police car? A forensic team?" Tania placed a particularly meaningful stress on the last. "Tell me there's not something odd going on."

"So what if there is? We aren't involved. It's not one of your bedside whodunnits."

"Oh, don't tell me you're not the tiniest bit intrigued."

"I know what it is," said Ron, stopping and turning to face his wife. "You've got the bit between your teeth after the Cornwall case, and you're trying to make a mysterious mountain out of a molehill so that you can play detective again."

"Nothing of the kind," retorted Tania. "I just want to be able to reassure Jenny that there's nothing going on."

"Oh, so that's what it is," grinned Ron. "Forgive me if I reply 'Yes, dear'."

"Anyway," said Tania with dignity. "I thought we might enjoy a pleasant lunch together. And if there's anything to know, Sharon Burley will be able to tell us."

"Of that I'm certain," said Ron, as the pair entered the abbey and made their way towards the Holy Grail.

There was an element of strain in the smile with which Sharon greeted Tania and Ron. "Hello again, you two. We don't usually see you twice in one week."

"Ah well, special circumstances," replied Tania.

Sharon's face grew solemn. "Oh. You've heard, then."

"We've heard the bare bones," said Tania. "Somebody's died, and there's already gossip going about town, so I thought the best person to give us the actual facts would be you."

"You're not the only ones to think that," said Sharon with a grim smile. "I've been rushed off my feet this morning with people I've never seen before in my life, although they've obviously been locals, because they've all enquired, oh so casually, as they order a tea, if there's anything interesting happening around the abbey at the moment. I've just been putting everybody off with a smile and a shrug. I haven't had the time to sit down, never mind indulge in idle speculation with total strangers."

"At least it seems to have quietened down at the moment," observed Ron as he surveyed the otherwise empty café.

"Thank goodness," said Sharon.

"And, believe it or not, we have actually come in for some lunch," continued Ron. "Although," he added with an impish smile, "if you happened to let slip anything about the current situation, we wouldn't object."

Sharon, almost against her instincts, returned a rather wan version of the smile. "Oh, I don't mind telling you two. You're friends. But first things first. Let me take your order, and then we'll see."

Some minutes later, with food and drinks ordered and delivered, Tania indicated a spare chair at the couple's table. "Come on, Sharon. You might as well take advantage of the fact that there's nobody else here to sit down for a minute. You can bring us up to date as we eat."

Sharon took the offered seat. "It was about five minutes before the abbey was due to close last night," she began. "And I'm not normally here that late, but I'd had one or two things to do, and I realised that the big oven was desperately in need of a clean, so I thought I might as well get on and do it while the place was quiet. Anyway, here I was, head in the oven, and I thought I heard a scream. I couldn't be sure, because the door tends to muffle things, so I went out into the church, and there was Louise Froyle – you know, the woman in charge of the flower arrangements ..."

"Oh, we know Louise," nodded Tania. "She did the flowers on the altar when we got married."

"And don't ask how long ago that was," put in Ron. "But she was an old lady even then."

"And still going strong, for all that she's eighty-odd," said Sharon. "Not that she was looking particularly strong last night. Proper shaken up, she was. Good thing I was here. I brought her in and made her a cup of good strong tea."

"So what had actually happened?" enquired Tania.

"We don't really know. Everybody seemed to appear at once from all directions, and there was Louise standing by the body. Professor Langley it was, the one the bishop had sent to assess the book. And he was lying there, under the edge of the museum parapet - he'd obviously fallen from above, somehow."

"Like I almost did," said Ron to Tania, with a shiver. "When we were up there to see the new display."

"But the horrible thing was," continued Sharon, "it looked as if he'd fallen straight on to his head. I mean, I didn't look too closely, but it seemed as if it was all crushed, and there was blood and some other stuff I don't like to think about." She shuddered. "We were all sure that he was dead, but somebody had to take a look, and being as I'm a registered first-aider, it had to be me. I just checked for a pulse on his wrist, and there was nothing. Then the rector said we'd better ring for an ambulance anyway, and everyone just sat there waiting for it to come while I brought Louise in here. And then the ambulance came, and a few minutes after that, a police car turned up, and they started asking questions."

"Sounds ghastly," remarked Ron.

"But the thing is, Tania," said Sharon, turning a face of appeal towards the librarian. "I can't believe that it was just a simple accident. I mean, if the professor was up there on his own, why should he suddenly fall? There's been things going on, and it doesn't seem right to me. There's been an atmosphere, all of a sudden. So ..."

"So ...?" Tania had an uneasy feeling that she knew what was coming.

Sharon took a deep breath. "You worked out what happened when that chap died when you were down in Cornwall doing the play, didn't you?"

"I suppose so," admitted Tania.

"You know you were streets ahead of the police, love," declared Ron robustly. "You ferreted out the truth when nobody else could. And if Sharon thinks there's something amiss ..."

"But why would you think that, Sharon?" asked Tania. "You say things have been going on. What do you mean? What sort of things?"

"I've heard stuff," said Sharon. She drew her chair closer to the table. "For instance ..."

"Yes?"

"Well, for a start, I know that professor ... person ..." A curl of the lip. "... was out to cause trouble. You see, I'd thought it would be nice to take him up a pot of tea and a bite to eat while he was working up in the museum, just to be friendly. Huh! I wish I hadn't bothered. Because later on he brought the tray back down with the tea not touched, and one bite out of one of my best pastries. One bite, mark you! I thought, how rude! But I didn't say anything, because he had Peter Hawkley with him at the time, and I didn't want to make a fuss, so I just took the stuff back into the wash-up to clear the things away. Well! Fuss? I needn't have worried."

"How come?" said Tania, intrigued.

"Because no sooner was I out of the way, than this Langley chap rounded on Peter. Because Peter had apparently asked him what he thought of the guided tour he'd given him, and the professor couldn't have been ruder. He told Peter in no uncertain terms that he thought his talk on the abbey and its history was so much rubbish. Well, you can imagine. Poor Peter was quite taken aback. He asked what was wrong with it, and Mr So-called Professor said he didn't know where to start. He said the history was all wrong, the descriptions of the architecture were complete gibberish, and Peter's ... what did he call it? Oh yes ... 'narrative style' ... would bore anybody to death before they got halfway round."

"Whew! Didn't pull his punches, then, this Langley chap," remarked Ron.

"Not so's you'd notice," agreed Sharon drily. "But worse still, the professor said that, in his opinion, to do the abbey justice, the only thing to do would be to engage a firm of professional guides for the future, and he would be making his recommendation to the bishop accordingly. And then he just walked out."

"How dreadful for Peter," said Tania. "How did he take it?"

"Not well, as you can imagine," replied Sharon. "Because as soon as I heard the door slam behind the professor, I came back out, and there was Peter standing there with his mouth just opening and closing, like a fish out of water. So I just said, gently-like, would he like a cup of tea, but he said no, he really ought to get back to his desk because he didn't like to leave it unattended for too long. And off he went. But he was shaken, I could tell."

"That's appalling," said Ron. "Langley had no right

to talk to anyone like that."

"Oh, poor Peter wasn't the only one to get the rough edge of that man's tongue," said Sharon. "There's more than one person who got the benefit of his lordship's opinion."

"Really?" asked Tania. "Who's that?"

"Heather," replied Sharon shortly.

"Not Heather who runs the little shop by the exit?" Ron sounded disbelieving. "But she's such a nice person. And she has some charming things in that shop of hers."

"Not according to the high and mighty Professor Langley, she doesn't," said Sharon grimly.

"So how do you know this?" enquired Tania. "What happened?"

"It was yesterday," explained Sharon. "I was taking a cup of tea ... I seem to do that a lot, don't I? ... up to Adrian Hinton in the organ loft, because I'd noticed he was up there practising for something or other, and I know it gets a bit chilly round the abbey in the evenings, because we can't afford to keep the heating on all the time, what with the price of fuel and everything. Anyway, I was on my way up to see him, and I saw Heather. It looked as if she'd just come down from the direction of the museum, and I thought she seemed a bit upset, so I asked her if there was anything wrong, and she said no and just put her head down and carried on towards her shop. About twenty past eight, that must have been."

"Okay. And then ..." encouraged Sharon.

"Well, of course, I didn't believe her for a second, so as soon as I'd dropped off Adrian's tea I went down to the shop to see how she was doing, only to find the poor woman in floods of tears."

"And did she say why?"

"Oh, eventually, when she could string two words together. She told me that she'd asked that damned professor ... excuse my language ... if he could give her some advice as to what she ought to be selling in her shop. Because, you know, she cares that it makes a contribution to the running costs of the abbey, so she always wants to do her best for the place."

"And I'm guessing that Professor Langley's words were not exactly encouraging," deduced Ron.

"I tell you, if he'd said such things to me I'd have given him a thick ear," declared Sharon hotly. "He told Heather, in so many words, that her stock was a load of rubbish. And I don't think 'rubbish' was the word he used, except that Heather was too much of a lady to repeat what he said. He described her souvenirs as the worst kind of overpriced tourist tat. He said that her cuddly teddy bear nuns, which the children love, ought to be burned at the stake, and if she was going to be selling books, she ought to aim for people with a reading age of over five. Which is what he assumed hers was, having chosen what was on offer. I'll tell you one thing. If he'd spoken to me like that, I would have had the greatest pleasure in going up to that museum and pushing him over the edge myself."

"Oh, you're surely not saying that Heather would ever be capable of doing such a thing," said Tania. "From what I know of her, she's the nicest person imaginable."

"It's amazing what some people are driven to under extreme pressure," Ron reminded her darkly. "You only have to cast your mind back to past events."

"But even so ..."

At that moment, the door to the café opened, and a young couple ushered a trio of boisterous children into the room. "Can we get something to eat here?" enquired the woman.

"Of course," said Sharon, leaping to her feet and swiftly taking up her place behind the counter. "Talk to me later," she mouthed to Tania. "There's more." She turned to the new arrivals. “Now, what can I get you?”

Chapter 9
Thursday

"It sounds," said Ron to his wife in confidential tones, "as if the professor was not an especially pleasant man."

"Putting it mildly," agreed Tania. "I can't understand why somebody would go out of their way to be unkind to perfectly nice people. It almost sounds as if he was revelling in it."

"But it's still no good reason for someone to kill him," pointed out Ron. "If that's what happened. We still don't have any evidence to indicate anything of the kind."

"Except for Sharon's instinct. She said there's been an atmosphere. Maybe it boiled over into something."

"And the only way you're going to find out the truth," said Ron, "is by doing what you do best. Talk to people. So shall we be about it?" He rose to his feet and held the chair for Tania, and the two, with a brief wave of farewell to the café manageress, headed for the door.

As Tania and Ron emerged from the Holy Grail and entered the nave of the abbey, they looked to one side to see Cassandra Milton rising from her knees at the altar rail. She turned and, noticing the visiting couple, moved towards them, a wan smile on her face.

Tania held out her hands. "Rector," she said, "we've just heard the terrible news about what happened last night from Sharon. It must have come as a dreadful shock."

"It was," said Cassandra simply.

"Sharon told us that there were several people here when the body was found. Were you one of them?"

"I was. I'd been in the vestry – I'd had an appointment at eight to talk with a couple about their wedding plans - and I came out when I heard Louise scream, and then we found poor Tarquin."

"So you hadn't seen him fall?"

"Nobody had. We don't know what happened. That's what I told the police when they came. That was after the ambulance crew had confirmed that he was dead, of course, but then everything went into limbo because they called in some forensic people. Not that there was anything for them to find, of course. The leading woman went up to look at the museum, but she said that, as far as she could detect, there were no indications as to how Tarquin might have fallen. No signs of a scuffle or marks on the rail at the edge of the parapet, so she was satisfied that there was nothing to show that anyone else was involved. She was planning to report that the simplest explanation seemed to be an unfortunate accident, and the police detective was happy to fall in with her assessment. And then they took the body away for further examination, just to be sure." Cassandra shook her head as if bewildered. "I can't see how such a thing could have happened to Tarquin."

"I notice you call him 'Tarquin'," ventured Tania. "Was that because you knew him before? Were you friends?"

A slight reserve seemed to enter the rector's manner. "I suppose you could say that. He was on the teaching staff at Camford University when I was a student there."

"Oh, I see. One of the lecturers. And that's when you were friends?"

"Yes." Cassandra was plainly reluctant to go into any further details. "But I haven't seen him for many years."

"But nevertheless ..." Tania left the sentence hanging. "Our sympathies, of course." Ron nodded in agreement.

At that moment, the sound of abbey clock could

be faintly heard striking the hour. Tania looked at her watch. "Heavens, is it that time already? I should be back at work. We'd better be going, Ron." And with a farewell smile to the rector, the couple made their way back out into the Market Square.

"There's something she's not telling us," said Ron, as the two prepared to part at the door of the library.

"Absolutely," agreed Tania. "I'm more than ever convinced that Sharon's instincts are right."

"So what are you going to do about it?" smiled Ron.

"I'm going to carry on talking to people," said Tania. "Starting tomorrow. What a good job the library closes on a Friday."

"Aha!" Ron gave a grin. "I detect a 'bit between the teeth' moment. But in the meantime, you'd better get back to work, or you won't have a job to have a day off from. Go!" A quick peck on the cheek, and Ron headed off across the Market Square as Tania made her way into the building.

*

"Honey, I'm home!" came the cry as the front door closed.

Ron emerged smiling from the kitchen. "Isn't that all rather counter-intuitive, love?" he enquired. "Aren't I, as the traditional bread-winning husband, supposed to come in from work with that greeting, as you, the conventional housewife, appear apron-clad to tell me that my supper is on the table?"

Tania joined in with the smile. "And whoever said we set out to be a conventional couple?"

"Nobody in my hearing, love," admitted Ron. "So you won't be surprised to learn that your supper is very much not on the table. In fact, I thought I'd give cooking a miss altogether this evening."

"So, what? We starve?"

"Certainly not. I just thought we might treat ourselves to a bite at the Cross Keys this evening," continued Ron. "They do a very good bar menu," he added with elaborate casualness.

Tania gazed at him with suspicion. "If I didn't know better, I'd think you were up to something."

"Me?" replied Ron with an appearance of outraged innocence. Tania gave him a look. "Okay," he capitulated. "You've got me. I simply thought, since you appear to be firmly settling into Miss Marple mode once again, that where better to try to pick up a few snippets than the pub? You know Dennis Dean always has his ear to the ground."

"You, husband mine, are extremely devious," chuckled Tania. "I knew there must be some reason I fell in love with you. And since you have clearly become a convert to my activities in the world of detection, I will fall in with your cunning plan. Once I've had a bath."

"I shall bring you up a glass of wine," said Ron. "And who knows? As I'm not tied to the kitchen, we shall have plenty of time before we need to go out, so perhaps, when you're feeling relaxed ..."

"Mr Faye, you are a very wicked man." Tania gave a smile which was not altogether discouraging as she began to climb the stairs.

*

"Good evening, Dennis." Tania gave a bright smile to the landlord of the Cross Keys as she perched on a bar stool. "How are things with you?"

"Oh, pretty decent, Mrs Faye, thanks very much. How's yourself?"

Tania thought for a moment before answering. "Intrigued at the moment, I suppose you could say."

"Oh yes?" Dennis raised an quizzical eyebrow. "That sounds as if it could be worth hearing about. But first, I'd better sort you out some drinks. What'll you have?"

"G and T for the good lady, and a pint of Ferret's Firkin for myself," said Ron. "And then I'm sure you'll be able to tempt us with something off your bar menu. Somehow or other, I seem to have worked up something of an appetite. Ow!" he added, as Tania elbowed him sharply in the ribs.

"Coming right up," replied Dennis.

Some while later, following the consumption of some very generous portions of scampi and chips and the pub's speciality treacle tart, Dennis returned to collect the empty plates, giving Tania an enquiring look. "Now, Mrs F, seeing as how I'm not too busy at this particular moment, I reckon I can delegate the running of this bar to my trusty staff, which means I can offer you a trade. You tell me what's 'intriguing' you, and I can let you in on what's been going on here."

"Now that sounds like a deal," said Ron. "So how about if I grab that table in the corner, you rustle us up a couple more drinks, together with one for yourself, of course, and we can swap stories."

As Dennis squeezed his formidable shape into a captain's armchair at the table where the Fayes were ensconced, he turned to Tania expectantly. "Now, bearing in mind what's gone on in Ramston in the last twenty-four hours, how far off the mark would I be if I guessed that your 'intrigued' has something to do with the abbey?"

Tania laughed. "Dennis, you are far too sharp. Of course it has."

"That didn't take much working out," said Dennis with a grin. "There's a sudden death just across the road, and next thing I know, our local Miss Marple turns up here looking all bright-eyed and innocent, just ready to pump the local pub landlord for information."

"Was I really so obvious?" asked Tania.

"I've never known you to make a beeline for me and perch yourself at the bar before now," replied Dennis. "Candlelight in the restaurant has always been your style."

"Well, thank you for that. And by the way, Miss Marple is a very elderly lady, so less of the Agatha Christie references, if you don't mind!"

"Fair enough," said Dennis, unabashed. "But you got to admit, you have got yourself something of a reputation round here with those of us in the know. So come on. Are you investigating this professor chap's death?"

"Very unofficially," insisted Tania. "Because from what I hear, the police seem to think that there's nothing odd about it. But I also hear that one or two things have been said which sound as if there were some undercurrents which the police don't know about."

Dennis nodded. "You couldn't be more right there. Of course, you know he was staying here? Well, supposed to be. He never got as far as his bed before he copped it, but there was plenty kicking off before that."

"Oh? How do you mean?"

"Well, for a start, he was booked in for supper at half-past six last night. Fine. And we'd also had that Miss Weston in for an early bite in the restaurant. You know her?"

"Pandora Weston? Yes, of course I do. She's one of the most borrowed authors from the library. And she's been in once or twice to give a talk and to do a book-signing. She's very well thought of."

"Oho! Not by everyone, it seems," stated Dennis. "Because she was finishing her meal just as Professor Langley arrived, and as it happened I'd seated them next to one another, and I just mentioned about her being an author and him being here to look into this book they've just found at the abbey, and I thought they might have some interests in common."

"And ...?"

"Not a bit of it. The professor more or less said that he didn't give two pins for her sort of books, and that she didn't have a clue when it came to writing history. Very snotty, he was. Well, you can imagine that didn't go down too well. She gave him such a glare, and then she stormed out, saying she was off to the abbey to sort things out for herself. Not what you'd call the friendliest encounter."

"And very much in tune with other conversations with other people that we've heard about," said Ron. "It sounds as if he couldn't help himself."

"And that wasn't the only person whose nose he got up last night," said Dennis. "You probably won't believe this, but he even had an up-and-downer with the rector."

"Cassandra Milton?" Tania sounded incredulous. "I don't believe it."

"I don't blame you. Not that I know her well, but she's always been thoroughly pleasant to me, and I've not heard a word said against her. Well, not till last night, anyway."

"Why, what happened?" enquired Ron.

"It was some time after seven, I reckon. That's right, because it would have been just after that early evening service they have at the abbey."

"Evensong."

"That's the one. I'm not really up on all these things," confessed Dennis, "not being much of a church-goer myself. I suppose some people would probably call me a bit of a heathen, but I ask you, when does a pub landlord ever get the chance to go to church, specially on a Sunday? Mind you, I do like the sound of the bells."

"So it was after evensong," prompted Tania, attempting to bring Dennis back on track.

"That's right. And I know that because we always get a bit of a bump in customers when they're turning out after the service. But what I didn't expect was that, a couple of minutes after the usual lot came in, the rector herself turned up. And she obviously knew the professor was staying here, and when she spotted him in the restaurant, she headed straight for him. And I wouldn't usually listen in to people having a private conversation, but as it happened, I was clearing away a couple of things that my staff had overlooked in the little corner booth where Miss Weston had been sitting, and I sort of got trapped in there, on account of I couldn't really make a move without them seeing me. I didn't want to embarrass the rector."

"But why would you have done that?" wondered Ron.

"Because the first thing she said to the professor," said Dennis, "was something like 'Don't think because we used to have a relationship that I won't do everything in my power to stop you'."

Tania's eyes widened. "She actually said 'relationship'?"

"Heard it with my own ears."

Tania turned to her husband. "I knew it! I said there was something she wasn't telling us. So obviously there was more than a teacher/student friendship going on."

"Sounds like it," agreed Ron. "So what else was said, Dennis?"

"I couldn't actually see Professor Langley from where I was sat, but I could hear a sort of sneer in his voice. And he said that it was a good thing this book had been found, whatever it turned out to be, because it gave a real history professional a chance to assess the abbey's excuse for a museum, which was nothing less than pathetic. There were one or two pieces worth looking at, but the rest was a mishmash of rubbish and irrelevancies, and as for the staffing, that was beyond a joke. He said the only sensible thing to do would be to close the whole lot down and transfer the exhibits to the proper museum at the cathedral in Westchester, lock, stock, and barrel."

"How did the rector react to that?"

"She actually sounded a bit choked up. And she said that she couldn't believe that what she'd once thought of as love could turn so poisonous. And she'd make sure that everyone, from the bishop down, knew what kind of man he had become. And he laughed."

Tania shook her head. "Laughed?"

"That he did. And he said to her, 'Don't bother to go running to the bishop with tales, my dear Cassandra. You won't be believed. As your knowledge of classical Greek mythology will surely tell you'."

"What?" Ron sounded puzzled. "What on earth was he drivelling on about?"

"Cassandra was a character in Greek mythology," explained Tania. "During the Trojan war. Granted the gift of prophecy by the gods, but cursed by never being believed."

"And how did she react to that?"

"She went very quiet," said Dennis. "And then she said, 'Take my word for it, Tarquin. I can quote history just as well as you. Remember what happened to the last King of Rome. One way or another, you will be stopped'. And then she turned on her heel and left, and I took my chance to sidle out. And the professor himself went off about half an hour later, and that was the last I saw of him."

"Sounds as if you had an eventful evening, one way or another," remarked Ron.

"Oh, that weren't the end of it," said the landlord with a wry smile. "Because later on, much nearer closing time, we had another little situation. Oh, nothing like the others. But that woman who runs the shop over at the abbey ... I can't remember her name ..."

"Heather Clanville?"

"Probably. Like I say, I don't really know her, but I do know the friend she came in with, because she's one of my regulars. And this friend, she brought Heather in, cooing over her because she seemed all of a doo-dah. So when Caroline – that's the friend – came up to the bar, I asked her if there was something up, and she said her friend had had a shock, and she'd asked Caroline to come and pick her up from work. Turns out this friend's mother used to run the abbey shop before Heather, and she said there'd been some sort of kerfuffle over at the abbey which had upset Heather no end."

"That fits in with what we'd already heard from Sharon," said Tania in an aside to Ron.

"Now I don't know what was said between them, of course, and I didn't want to pry, so I didn't ask any more questions but just dispensed a couple of large medicinal brandies. And after a bit, the two ladies left. But obviously, the upset was all mixed in with the professor's death, which of course I got wind of when he never turned up overnight." Dennis cast a slightly guilty look around the bar. "Here, I'd better get on, otherwise my staff are going to start complaining about having to do all the work while I'm sat here nattering." He got to his feet. "But if anything else comes my way, I'll drop you the word."

"Thanks, Dennis," replied Tania. "And I'll return the compliment. We have to make sure you're up to speed, otherwise your reputation as the man who knows everything will be ruined."

"It will that," chuckled Dennis, and headed back to the bar.

"Well," said Ron, "you must be building up a nice

little dossier in your head."

"I think I am," said Tania. "We'd better get home so that I can make some notes before I forget everything."

"Remind me to buy you a policeman's notebook for your next birthday," grinned Ron. "I'm already looking forward to watching you carrying on with your sleuthing activities tomorrow."

Chapter 10
Friday

"So, what do we plan for today, love?" enquired Ron Faye through a mouthful of toast.

"We?" queried his wife, pouring a second cup of tea.

"I thought I might see if I can offer a morsel of assistance," replied Ron diffidently. "I can't expect you to carry the heavy burden of investigating a dastardly crime on your own." He grinned.

"That's if it is a dastardly crime. We're not absolutely certain that it is yet."

"But there are enough straws in the wind to make you wonder."

Tania nodded. "After what we heard yesterday, there are."

"So I'm happy to be your metaphorical bag-carrier," smiled Ron. "I shall follow three paces behind and make mental notes."

"Are you sure you can spare the time? Don't you have a living to earn? We do need to eat, you know," pointed out Tania.

"I can put everything on the back burner for a couple of days," Ron reassured her. "That's the beauty of working for myself. I've got no immediate deadlines staring me in the face, and I'll always have my phone to hand if anything crops up."

"In which case," smiled Tania, "welcome back aboard." She paused for a moment. "So, I've been thinking ..."

"Always dangerous," murmured Ron.

Tania ignored him. "... that there were other people around the abbey at the time of the ... whatever-it-was, accident or attack ... that we haven't spoken to yet. For a start, there was Louise Froyle who was the first one to come across the professor's body. She may have seen or heard something. And Sharon Burley told us she was taking a cup of tea to Adrian Hinton while he was doing his rehearsing in the organ loft. If he was around at the crucial time, he may have something to tell us."

"And don't forget," pointed out Ron, "Sharon herself said that she had more to say, except that she was interrupted when those people came into the café."

"That's true. In fact, there's a whole list of people that might be able to shed some light. We probably ought to talk to them all." Tania started ticking them off on her fingers. "There's the rector herself, plus Heather in the shop, and then Peter Hawkley the guide is always around somewhere, and of course I know Pandora Weston, so we'll have to go and see her ..."

"Whoa! Slow down!" cried Ron. "Let's not go mad. You'll run out of fingers any second. Let us approach this calmly."

"You're right," agreed Tania with a wry smile. "What do you suggest?"

"For a start, I intend to finish my breakfast. I may even have an extra piece of toast to fortify me for the strenuous activities ahead. And then we should stroll over to the abbey in a leisurely fashion, and casually engage in conversation with whoever happens to be around. Let's see where that takes us."

Tania leaned across to deposit a peck on her husband's cheek. "You were always the clever one."

"Simple application of management skills," replied Ron. "Now ... toast."

*

As Tania and Ron approached the Jerusalem Porch, they encountered Louise Froyle almost buried under the profusion of flowers she carried.

"Goodness, Louise," exclaimed Tania, "can you manage all those on your own? Do let us help you."

"I wouldn't say no," replied Louise with some relief, as she unloaded several bunches of blooms on to both Tania and Ron. "It's all right until I get to the door, but sometimes it's closed when I get to it, and it's so heavy I have to wait for somebody to come and let me in." And as Ron managed to manhandle the sturdy nail-studded oaken door and hold it open for the three, "Lucky you came along. It's just down here." She led the way down the side aisle to one of several small chantry chapels tucked away behind their screens of fretted stonework, this one furnished with buckets, vases in a variety of styles, wrought-iron stands, and watering-cans, to provide the most unusual flower room Tania had ever seen. With a slight sigh, she laid her burden down on a trestle table and indicated to the others to do likewise.

"It looks as if you're going to be very busy today, Louise," remarked Tania as she surveyed the floral array.

"You know what they say? No rest for the wicked," said Louise with a wheezy chuckle. "But I do like to keep the abbey looking nice. And we've got a wedding this afternoon, so there's a bit of extra special work to be done."

"But not all on your own, surely?" said Ron.

"Oh no. I've got some of the other ladies coming in to help me set everything up a bit later. But I like to be the one who buys the flowers and decides what the colour themes and the arrangements are going to be. Course, for weddings I always talk it over with the bride, like that nice young couple who came in to see the rector on that dreadful evening. It's my little project. And it gives me something to do. And that florist on the corner of the Square, he gives me special prices for the abbey flowers, and once in a while he even makes up a little extra bouquet for me, on the house, he says, just to say thank you for the custom. After all, I'm in there most days."

"And it sounds as if you're in here all the hours God sends," observed Tania.

"Well, at least it means I shall be in the right place when the Lord decides to send for me," chuckled Louise. "And I can be sure I'll have some lovely flowers for my funeral," she added with a twinkle.

"Speaking of funerals," said Tania, seizing the opportunity which Louise's remark gave, "I gather it was you who were first on the scene when Professor Langley's body was found."

"That I was," nodded Louise solemnly. "And a right turn it gave me."

"What exactly happened?" asked Ron.

"I'd been sat in here," began Louise, "because I was just getting ready to do what I usually do, which is to go all round the flower arrangements during the evening, just before the abbey closes, to do a bit of dead-heading, so as to make sure everything will be looking nice when we open up the next morning. And I'd looked in on Saint George, but his roses were still absolutely beautiful, because if there's one thing you can say about roses, they do last a good long time. So, I'd done that, and I was going round in a sort of circuit which took me up to the west end, underneath the tower, and there he was! Sprawled on the stones, right underneath where the museum is up above, so it was obvious to me that he'd fallen from there. And I'm sorry if it sounds a bit grizzly, miss, but dead-heading wasn't the half of it. He'd clearly fallen straight on to his head, and it was all smashed in, with blood and all-sorts. Not that I wanted to stare too closely, but I couldn't help noticing. So then I let out a scream, and everybody came running from all directions, and then Sharon came and took me into the café and made me sit down with a good strong cup of sweet tea. For the shock, she said, and it turns out she was right, because I did feel better, for all that I never take sugar in my tea normally. And while that was happening, I think they telephoned for an ambulance ... not that it would have done the professor much good from what I saw, but I suppose they had to try ... and they said the police came along after that."

"So you didn't see or hear anything of what went on afterwards?" queried Tania.

"Afterwards? No. But before? Oh, that's another matter," grunted Louise.

Tania and Ron exchanged glances. "Before?" enquired Tania. "How do you mean?"

Louise pulled a face. "Now I'm not normally one to speak ill of the dead," she said. "But that professor, it seems to me that he was quite a nasty piece of work."

"What makes you say that?" asked Ron.

"Our rector, she's a wonderful woman," said Louise. Tania wrinkled her brow in puzzlement at the elderly woman's apparent non-sequitur. "Now, I know there were some who weren't sure that she was right for the job when she first came here, but she proved them all wrong, and now you won't hear a word said against her round the town. Everybody respects her. Well, I say everybody. Not that professor. I've never heard anybody speak to her the way he did."

"When was this?" wondered Tania. "And what was it that he said?"

"It must have been about an hour before I found him, so maybe about half-past eight on Wednesday evening. You see, I'd tried something new with the altar decorations and I wanted to see how it looked from the far end of the nave, so I was standing there at the back. Actually, it was almost exactly on the spot where ..." Louise shuddered. "Oh, it's really strange to think of it, that not an hour later, he'd be lying there dead. Anyway, I saw the rector come out of the vestry, after that young couple had left, and she came up that side of the church and made for the stairs up to the museum. I don't think she noticed me. But as I stood there, I could hear voices drifting down over the balcony, and it was the rector talking to the professor. Now I don't normally like to eavesdrop, but I couldn't help hearing. She said to him that she really didn't want to cause trouble, because her job was to be a peacemaker above everything, but he said 'Do your worst, Cassie dear'. Honestly! 'Cassie'! What a way to speak to her. And he went on that if she stood in his way, he wouldn't hesitate to spill the beans about her past to the bishop. He said 'I'm sure he'd be fascinated to hear about the scandalous personal history of the woman he's put in charge of this place. Because I'm sure I can't have been your only one. Student morals being what they are'. And she said that it was all so long ago, and things were different, and he laughed and said 'Mud sticks, my dear. Let's see how you survive that'. And I thought, I'm not going to stand there and listen to any more of this nastiness, so I came back here. But I was all of a tremble."

"And you don't know what it was the professor was referring to?"

"I do not," said Louise stoutly. "And what's more, I don't want to know. I'm not one to pry. I speak as I find, and our rector is a credit to the abbey and a fine woman, and that's good enough for me."

"It does sound as if our Professor Langley was prone to a little blackmail in pursuit of his ends," remarked Ron to Tania.

"A little?" Louise sounded outraged. "Oh, I could tell you a thing or two," she snorted.

"You mean there was someone else he threatened?" asked Tania.

"Yes," said Louise, "and you'll never believe who. That nice young Robin Barton."

"Robin, the teacher at the Abbey School? I know

him," said Tania. "He comes into the library every so often."

"Is there anyone you don't know?" murmured Ron in his wife's ear.

Tania ignored her husband. "But what on earth could Robin Barton have done to fall foul of Tarquin Langley?"

"I think it was the other way around," replied Louise. "Now, I don't know if you know, but Robin ..." She seemed to be searching for words. "He's got a friend ..."

Tania smiled. "I think you mean his husband Tom," she said. "They come into the library together. They're a lovely couple, and everyone I know likes them. So if you're thinking there's some sort of secret that Robin's trying to keep, you couldn't be further from the mark."

"Oh. Right. That's good. But don't forget, I'm an old woman," pointed out Louise. "Some things take a bit of getting used to at my age. As long as they're happy, I suppose. Now, you know Robin's one of our bell-ringers?"

"I didn't, but carry on," said Ron.

"So they had a rehearsal the other night, the night of the accident. Finished at eight like always, they did. And they all left, but Robin came back a few minutes later. I was talking to Peter Hawkley at his desk when Robin re-appeared because he said he'd forgotten something, so he nipped back up the stairs towards the ringing chamber. But then he didn't come back down for several minutes, so I wondered if something was up, and I was just going to get in the lift to go up to check, because my knees aren't what they used to be, when I heard voices echoing down the spiral stairs. It's the stone, you see. It amplifies the noise. And the voices were Robin and this professor. And I couldn't believe my ears."

"Why?"

"Because that nasty professor, he seemed to be trying it on with Robin. He said he knew all about him, and if Robin didn't come to his hotel room that night, he was going to put it about that Robin had been up to things he shouldn't have with one of the choirboys. And Robin said that the idea was ridiculous, and nobody who knew him would believe a word of it, but the professor said that most people would say that there's no smoke without fire, and wouldn't it be better to save his reputation as a teacher by making just one small sacrifice. 'After all, dear boy, it's not as if it's anything you haven't done before', he said. Disgusting man! And Robin just said 'Don't you ever touch me again', and he came clattering down the stairs, and I only just managed to get out of the way in time so that he didn't see me."

"I think," mused Ron, "that Professor Langley seems to have had a profound talent for making enemies. You know, if his death wasn't an accident, we seem to be amassing a fine crop of motives."

Louise was agog. "Do you mean the police are saying it wasn't an accident? Somebody killed him?"

Tania shook her head. "I haven't heard anything of the sort. And I've got access to some of the finest gossips in Ramston," she added with a smile.

"Well, if somebody did bump him off, I wouldn't blame them too much," muttered Louise. "Not if that's the way he was going on. I suppose I'm one of the lucky ones, not getting on the wrong side of him. Mind you, if he'd come round criticising my flower arrangements, I'd have told him where to go in no uncertain terms."

"I bet you would, Louise," grinned Ron. "I don't think I'd be too eager to get on the wrong side of you myself."

"Oh, go on with you," said Louise, giving him an unexpected playful push. Her face sobered. "Mind you, that man could have been saying all sorts of things behind my back. I mean, I wouldn't be the only one."

"Oh?" Tania was intrigued.

"Oh yes. Because even if he wasn't up in people's faces, he didn't seem to have a good word to say about anyone."

"How do you mean?" enquired Ron.

"Well, you know Peter, the chief guide," said Louise. "Always as helpful as you please. It's down to him, more than anybody, that people put such lovely comments in the visitors' book about how welcoming the abbey is. He's always going out of his way to show people all the best points of interest so's they get the most out of their visit. And when that professor was here, Peter made a point of giving him the full works, telling him about this and that all round the building. I saw them set off. Proper proud of our abbey, is Peter. So anyway, he took the professor all round, and at the end of it he went back to his desk, and the professor came past me in here, because I was sat quietly making a list of the flowers I'd need for this wedding today, and as he went by I heard him say to himself 'Well, that was a total waste of time. That man is useless. He'll have to go.' And I thought, that's not very nice after Peter's been good enough to give him his time. But no – ungrateful doesn't begin to cover it."

Ron, prompted by the distant sounds of the abbey clock striking the hour, looked at his watch. "Louise, we've kept you far too long, and I'm sure you have things to do."

"I do," nodded Louise. "And if I don't get these flowers unwrapped and some vases sorted out, my ladies will be in here pestering me for something to do."

"Then we'll let you get on," said Tania. "And as it's eleven o'clock, that sounds like the perfect time for Ron to treat me to elevenses in Sharon's café."

"Provided I'm allowed to have one of her famous

sticky buns with my tea," smiled Ron.

"You do realise that there are those who are surprised that you aren't the size of a horse, with your penchant for cake and buns," remarked Tania with mock severity.

"Let him enjoy himself," said Louise. "You're only young once."

"Young-ish," whispered Tania in an aside to her husband.

Louise turned back to her flowers. "Right. Let me see. Now, what have we got?" She scanned the table. "Oh."

"Problem?" asked Ron.

"My gardening gloves. Save my fingers from the thorns on the roses. They should be here." Louise sighed in exasperation. "Sorry, but it makes me cross when my ladies borrow them and don't put them back in the right place. Oh well. They'll turn up. Enjoy your tea." She busied herself taking the cellophane off the bunches of flowers, as Ron and Tania headed in the direction of the Holy Grail.

Chapter 11
Friday

Ron and Tania scanned the interior of the unexpectedly busy café in search of a table, finally spotting one tucked away half-behind a pillar in one corner.

"You grab that table, and I'll order," hissed Tania, and Ron hastened to obey as his wife made for the counter, where Sharon Burley was just finishing dispensing a tray full of refreshments to a mature woman who was evidently part of a young and boisterous family, the parents of whom were striving without great success to keep their offspring under control. "Look out, here comes Grandma," she heard the father say, which brought about an almost miraculous instant improvement in the children's behaviour.

"Good morning, Tania," said Sharon with her customary welcoming smile.

"Hello, Sharon." Tania glanced over her shoulder at the buzzing room. "You seem to be doing a roaring trade. I don't think I've ever seen you so packed."

Sharon lowered her voice. "I reckon it's all on account of the professor's death. I think the word's got around, so people have come to gawp at the scene. You know what rubber-neckers some folks can be. But I don't suppose I should complain. My till's been ringing all morning, so that'll do the abbey's finances no harm at all."

"Silver lining, and all that," remarked Tania.

"So, let's have your order, and I'll bring it over to your table."

A few minutes later, Sharon was depositing a tray laden with teapot and cups, together with two plates, each of which bore one of the café's signature buns.

"Sticky buns all round, is it, love?" observed Ron

with a smile. "So, next time you accuse me of having an addiction to cakes, just remember, let her without sin cast the first stone."

"Shush, Ron," commanded Tania. "This is all by way of a not-so-subtle bribe to Sharon. She told us she had more to tell about the goings-on with the professor, so I hoped to encourage her to spill the beans."

Sharon laughed. "No need for bribes, my dear. But just you hold on there for a second, and then I'll come and squeeze in there with you." She darted over to the counter and called into the kitchen. "Joyce, can you watch the place for a minute?" A middle-aged woman wielding a tea-towel emerged from the back room. "I'm just sitting down with my friends over there for a second." With a wordless nod, the other woman set about straightening the display cabinet of cakes, while Sharon made her way back to the corner and eased her generous frame into the spare chair.

"When we were in here before, you said there was more to tell," said Ron.

"And you'd already told us about some kind of a to-do between the professor and Heather Clanville," added Tania.

"Plus he'd had a go at Peter Hawkley, you said," Ron reminded her.

"I'm surprised there's anybody left on the abbey team who hasn't had their efforts torn apart by the professor," said Tania drily.

"Well, this was a bit different, on account of it wasn't one of our own people," said Sharon. "This time it was that historian chap who's friends with the rector."

"What, Rudolph Wheatley?"

"That's the one. And I know he's the one she goes to for advice sometimes about the history of the place. That's how come he was the one who wrote the visitor guide to the abbey."

"And from what we know, he's apparently very prominent in his field," said Ron.

"Not according to that professor. In fact," Sharon added with a small chuckle, "excuse the pun, but it sounded more as if he thought Mr Wheatley ought to be put out to pasture. Sorry," she said, as Ron cast his eyes heavenwards. "But the thing is," she hurried on, "from what they were saying, they've got history." She put her hand to her mouth. "Sorry. I've done it again. What I mean is, they've known each other a long time."

"Okay, we got that," smiled Tania. "So what was it that was said? And when?"

"It would have been sometime on Wednesday afternoon, but I couldn't say exactly when. I'd had to pop out to the shop across the Square because, for some reason, I was running low on milk, and I came back in and I saw the professor coming out of Heather's shop. And I think he must have been heading up to the museum when he ran into Mr Wheatley, who was just emerging from Saint George's chapel. Well, Saint Elfleda's, of course, these days. And the professor said something like 'What's this, Wheatley? Doing a little research so that you can make up more nonsense about the abbey's past? I've had a glance at your so-called history of the place, and it was all I could do to stop myself laughing'. And they weren't making any effort to keep their voices down, and you know how sound echoes around the church, so there was no way I could avoid hearing them. And Mr Wheatley said that, for all the years he'd known him, he'd never heard the professor give a good opinion of any other academic. And the professor said 'Academic? Is that what you're calling yourself? The plain truth, my dear chap, is that you've never forgiven me for being appointed to a professorship which you ludicrously thought should have been yours'. But Mr Wheatley just looked at him, contemptuous-like, and said the professor had always been vicious. And the professor said that then it wouldn't come as a surprise that he was going to suggest to the bishop that Mr Wheatley was completely unfit to have anything to do with the abbey in future. Sneered, he did, and then just swept past him and headed for the lift. And Mr Wheatley just looked daggers at his back as he left, and from the expression on his face, I wouldn't like to say what he was thinking."

"Sharon, that's shocking," said Tania. "I can't help wondering why the bishop seems to think so highly of the professor, that he sent him here to make his recommendations."

"Perhaps the bishop's got some dark secrets of his own, and Langley knew where the bodies were buried," muttered Ron, half seriously. "But at any rate, he won't be making any recommendations now, will he?"

*

Emerging from the Holy Grail, Tania did a virtual dance in the doorway as she came face-to-face with Adrian Hinton with mug in hand. "Adrian! We can't keep meeting like this," she laughed.

"We do seem to be making a habit of it, don't we?" replied Adrian. "I was just bringing back the mug that Sharon had brought me up earlier. I've been running through the music for this wedding we've got later."

"And it sounds as if Sharon makes a habit of bringing you tea when you're up rehearsing in that organ loft of yours."

"I think she reckons I need mothering," smiled Adrian. "And I'm not one to turn down a generous impulse."

"In fact," said Tania, seizing the moment, "don't I remember she did something of the kind the other evening – the evening Professor Langley died?"

"As it happens, yes, she did."

"So I wonder if you were here when it actually happened."

"No, I'd left by then. Probably just as well. The atmosphere around the place was just too poisonous for comfort."

"Really? You mean there were things going on?" enquired Tania guilelessly.

"Oh yes," said Adrian.

"So what exactly do you mean? You saw or heard something to do with the professor?"

"Both, actually. It started when I'd only just got here, which must have been around half-past seven, or maybe a bit later, because one of my assistants had done evensong.. And I realised that I didn't have all the music I needed, so I had to go up to the bell-ringing chamber to fetch it."

"Why on earth did you need to do that?" wondered Ron.

"Don't forget that what is now the museum used to be the organ loft," pointed out Adrian. "That's years ago, of course, before they put the organ in where it is now. But for some reason, nobody thought to move the music storage cupboards to the new location - not that there would be much room for them anyway, because I'm pretty much perched on a shelf, and the music cupboards are very large. Some of the older music folios are huge. But anyway, I had to traipse up to the ringing chamber where the bell-ringers were in the throes of a rehearsal - fortunately just with hand-bells, because when they're using the real thing up in the bell tower, you can't hear yourself think in the ringing chamber. Anyway, long story short, I'd grabbed what I needed and I was on my way down when I could hear what sounded like a row coming from the museum. Well, I confess, I'm as curious as the next person, so I earwigged to hear what it was all about."

"And what was it about?" prompted Tania.

"It was that woman who writes books – I've seen her about the place."

"Pandora Weston?"

"That's the one! She does historical novels, doesn't she? So I'm guessing that she'd been up in the museum to take a look at the rector's latest treasure. Maybe she's planning on writing a book about it. Anyway, it sounded as if Professor Langley had just arrived, because he said 'Are you still here?', and she snapped back 'Evidently!', and he said that he couldn't imagine what she hoped to gain from looking at the manuscript, because as far as he was concerned, she probably didn't have an original creative bone in her body, and he wouldn't be surprised if she lifted all her material from other writers. She'd have plenty to choose from. And she said 'How dare you accuse me of plagiarism?' and he said 'If the cap fits'. And she said that Sister Catherine was one of her proudest creations, and he said from what he'd heard, Sister Cat would be better named Sister Catastrophe. 'So perhaps, my dear Pandora,' he said, 'you ought to change your *nom-de-plume* to Pandora Hopeless!'. And he gave a sneering laugh, as if he'd just made the greatest joke ever. But she said 'You will regret those words, Langley', and it sounded as if she was about to leave, so I got out of the way quick, because I didn't want her to catch me eavesdropping."

"It sounds as if it was difficult not to," commented Ron. "We were speaking to Sharon at the café earlier, and she made a remark about how echoey the abbey is, so you probably hear all sorts of things that were not meant for you." He gave a glance sideways in the direction of his wife. "I ... er ... I don't suppose," he added tentatively, "you happen to have overheard anything else that might be relevant over the past couple of days?"

Adrian reflected for a moment. "Actually, yes."

"You mean some sort of argument between the professor and someone else? Not that it would come as anything of a surprise."

"It wasn't so much of an argument as a downright threat," replied Adrian.

"Who to?" asked Tania. "I mean, to whom?" Ron, at her side, repressed a grin at the librarian in his wife asserting itself.

"It was Rudolph Wheatley."

"Again?" murmured Ron softly into Tania's ear.

"You know him, don't you?" continued Adrian. "That friend of the rector's who wrote the abbey guide book."

"And organised the museum too. Yes, of course I know him," confirmed Tania.

"Well, it was about the museum that they were speaking. Although it was Professor Langley who was doing most of the speaking. Mr Wheatley just seemed to sit there."

"So how exactly did the professor threaten Rudolph?" enquired Tania. "Because it's the first time we've heard any mention of anything violent."

"Oh, it wasn't anything like that," Adrian hastened to explain. "In fact, from what I saw of him, the professor didn't seem to be exactly the type for physical action. No, I think his weapons of choice were words. Or maybe poison," he added reflectively.

"Or the two together?" suggested Ron. "Poisonous words?"

"That sounds about right," said Adrian. "You see, I'd finished my practice session at about nine, and I was taking my music back to stash it away in the cupboard up in the tower. And fortunately, by then it all sounded pretty quiet around the abbey, so I thought the ructions of earlier on must have died down, thank goodness. But as I was heading back up the side aisle, I could hear voices coming from one of the little chantry chapels, so I just stopped, meaning to go back round the long way, because I didn't want to barge into someone's conversation. I wondered if it might be Peter, but then I realised I'd just seen him going up the tower on his rounds."

"So the voices were Professor Langley and Rudolph?" said Tania.

"The professor, yes. Mr Wheatley wasn't saying much, but I could just glimpse him through the gaps in the stonework. And the professor was saying that it looked as if he'd probably done everything he could here, and he'd need to carry on his work back in Camford, but as far as the abbey was concerned, he was finished. 'Funny, that, Rudolph,' he said, 'because much the same applies to you.' And Mr Wheatley asked what he meant, in a really tired sort of voice, and the professor said that the abbey's history as presented by Mr Wheatley's book and the display at the museum, as well as Peter's guiding, was nothing short of incompetent, and that he would be telling the bishop that the matter ought to be in the hands of real professionals. And Mr Wheatley said 'Like yourself, I suppose?', and the professor just replied 'If you like'. And Mr Wheatley said 'And what if I don't like? Because while there's breath in my body, you'll never succeed in hurting this place, or those who love it.' The professor just gave a sort of laugh and started to leave, and I ducked behind a pillar just in time. I didn't see what either of them did after that, because I sidled round to the other side of the church and went up to the music store that way."

"It sounds as if you managed to overhear more than enough to show us what sort of man the professor was," remarked Ron. "That's as if we were any doubt after what everyone else has told us," he added to Tania.

"So, with a bit of luck, Adrian, that's an end to what you heard."

Adrian nodded. "You could say that, I suppose." He paused as if uncertain. "Mind you, there was one other thing ..."

"Meaning ...?" prompted Tania.

"It wasn't so much what I heard as what I saw," said Adrian. "And I suppose I could have been mistaken, but I don't think so."

"So what was it?"

"It was not long after the bell-ringers had finished their practice. I remember that, because although they were only using the hand-bells that time, the sound does still carry, and it can be a bit off-putting if I'm trying to master a tricky section of music that I haven't played before. But anyway, they'd finished a few minutes earlier, and I reached a natural pause in the music, and I happened to glance up the church towards the museum, to see the professor and Robin Barton in conversation."

Tania raised her eyebrows. "Conversation?"

Adrian gave a wry smile. "Okay, so maybe that's the wrong word. They were speaking, let's put it that way, but from the body language, it didn't seem all that friendly. Obviously I couldn't hear, but I saw the professor go close up to Robin and put his hand on him, and then Robin shook the hand off and stepped back. He seemed angry, and then he left abruptly, and that was it."

"I think we may have an idea of what was happening then, from what someone else has told us," said Tania. "But I think we'd probably better leave it at that."

"Right," said Adrian. He suddenly seemed to realise that he was still holding the empty tea mug. "Lord, I really ought to get this back to Sharon. I seem to have been stood here for ages, and I'd better carry on getting ready for today's wedding. And there's another one tomorrow."

"Then we'd best not keep you," said Ron, as Adrian disappeared through the door of the Holy Grail. "Come on, love. I'm sure there'll be other people who need to be making preparations, so they won't want us cluttering the place up. Plus, don't forget we've got rehearsal tonight, and I was hoping we could go through our lines this afternoon. Leah said it's 'books down' this evening, and I don't want to run the risk of having to take prompts left, right, and centre."

"Good thinking," said Tania, somewhat reluctantly at being dragged away from her investigations.

"And just to be lazy," continued Ron, "how about we skip cooking and treat ourselves to fish and chips for lunch? We can have one of the Friday specials from the 'Tasty Plaice'."

"You know how to treat a girl," laughed Tania, and the couple made their way out into the sunlit Market Square.

Chapter 12
Friday

"'*Goodbye! Parting is such sweet sorrow!*' And exit. Curtain!"

"Well done, you," said Tania, sitting back and closing her script. "That, my darling, was practically word perfect."

"For which relief, much thanks," quipped Ron, "although 'practically perfect' may not cut it with Leah. You know what a stickler she is for accuracy with lines. Especially with a Noël Coward play, and even more because 'Blithe Spirit' is one of the most iconic."

"And her favourite. But I don't think you've got a thing to worry about. I'm sure there are going to be people rockier than you on script. But just remember one thing."

"And what's that?"

"For goodness' sake, don't actually say that last line of yours before the dress rehearsal."

Ron laughed. "Good thought. It's funny. To look at her, nobody would suspect a rugged no-nonsense Scotswoman to be in the least superstitious, but Leah is always absolutely adamant about sticking to the 'no final line during rehearsals' tradition. And as for quoting from 'The Scottish Play' ..." He pulled a face of feigned horror.

"Perhaps it's because she *is* Scottish," surmised Tania. "They say that there are some weird things go on up in the mists of the Highland glens."

"Which, considering she's from Glasgow, doesn't quite cut it," grinned Ron. "Well, this isn't getting the babby washed, as my old granny used to say." He heaved himself out of his armchair. "I for one could do with a cup of tea and a biccie, and then I suppose we'd better get ready for rehearsal. Time's wingèd chariot, and all that."

"And there would have been plenty of time for

everything," pointed out Tania with a smile and a faint blush, "if you hadn't had certain nefarious activities in mind this afternoon."

"So sue me," retorted an unrepentant Ron. "Just because I decided to have a well-earned siesta after lunch, nobody forced you to join me. And it wasn't my fault we fell asleep afterwards."

"Get that kettle on!" instructed Tania with mock severity. "Or we shall never get out!"

*

At the Waite Theatre, the former small cinema in the heart of Ramston which had been purchased through the efforts of the members of the Ramston Operatic And Dramatic Society and converted into their home and performance venue, Tania and Ron were greeted by an effervescent Susannah Talbot, who bounded down from the stage as they entered the auditorium.

"I know all my lines," declared the teenage girl excitedly. "Mum and dad took me through them when I got home from college, and I didn't make any mistakes."

"I don't see any reason why you should," replied Tania. "You were fine as Puck when we were down in Cornwall, and that's a much bigger part."

"I suppose so," said Susannah. "I don't have anywhere near so much script as I did in 'Midsummer Night's Dream', but ..." She adopted a brave smile. "... I am only playing the maid in this, after all."

"Don't do yourself down," said Ron. "You're crucial to the plot, don't forget. Without you, the whole play falls apart. And you've got some great comedy. You'll probably steal the show."

"Over my dead body!" declared Tania in counterfeit outrage.

"Speaking of which," said Ron, scanning the rest of the cast who were grouped on stage, "where is our Elvira? I can't be expected to rehearse without the ghost of my first wife."

"Esther? Oh, she's on her way," replied Susannah. "She just texted Leah to apologise. Paul's car wouldn't start. But she'll be here in time for her first entrance."

At this point Leah Sutherland, the play's director, in her customary check shirt, dungarees and sturdy biker boots, strode on to stage from the wings. She clapped her hands. "Right, everybody. Can I have your attention for a moment." The company obediently fell silent. "As you can see, David Kent and his team have made a giant leap with the set, so we've actually got all our doors and walls in place. However, please don't be too robust with the doors, as there's still some bracing to go on to make everything solid. Now, Sarah and Timothy have gathered together most of the props, although there are still a few bits and pieces left to find. And try not to be too disappointed, Madame Arcati, when you find that your gin is still only water." A quiet ripple of amusement ran around the company, while Tania feigned shock at the suggestion. "And all the necessary props for the first scene are in position on stage, with everything else on the props table stage left, for you to collect as needed. And I would remind you," she added with a note of severity, "that it is your responsibility to check your own props before we start. Yes?"

"Yes, Leah," came the chorused response. The company were well acquainted with Leah's strict approach.

"So," continued the director, "let's make a start. It's a full run-through, and may I remind you that I do not expect to see anyone with a script in their hand."

"What if someone dries?" enquired Martha Talbot, Susannah's mother. "Will anybody be prompting?"

"In the unlikely event of anyone needing a prompt," replied Leah with emphasis, "I shall be out front, and I will feed you the line." She looked around the cast. "I do not expect to be required to do so."

The members of the company exchanged looks of varying degrees of trepidation.

"By the way," said Leah, "as some of you may know, Esther has been delayed, but she has assured me that she will arrive before her first entrance. So we will begin. Places for the first scene please." The director made her way down to the first row of the stalls and seated herself, notebook in hand and pencil poised, while the members of the cast dispersed. "And we won't be using the curtains for this run, and we'll take our break at the end of Act 2, Scene 1. Stand by Edith and Ruth, and ... go!"

*

"Now before you all rush off to the canteen for your cup of tea," announced Leah, forestalling a general move towards the stairs down to the refreshment bar, "I have a few notes for you."

The slight sigh of resignation from the cast was almost inaudible.

"Not too many," continued the director, "because generally that went fairly well. But ... nothing is so good that it cannot be improved by a few tweaks. So ... Doctor and Mrs Bradman." Peter and Martha Talbot looked up expectantly. "I think you can go further with your characters. Mrs B, you can be even more twittery, and Doctor B, let's have a touch more amused scepticism. You're the last person to put up with quackery, don't forget." The couple nodded. "And Edith ..." Susannah's face demonstrated unease at what might be coming. "Very good ..." Susannah visibly relaxed. "... but I think you can huff and puff just a little as you're running about."

"Yes, Leah," replied a relieved Susannah.

"Now Ruth ..." Elizabeth Kent looked faintly

surprised at being called upon. "I like what you're doing, but I think we can have a touch more of the sharp claws at odd moments. Take a look through your lines and pick a few appropriate spots. And as for Charles ..."

"Yes, ma'am," responded Ron.

"The level of sophistication is pitched just about right, so I'm pleased with that, but I think you could add a mannerism which might help. You remember how Prince Philip tended to go about with one hand tucked in his jacket pocket? Not all the time, but occasionally. If you can wear a jacket for rehearsal, you can give that a try."

"I'll pop down to wardrobe and grab one from there."

"Good. And while you're at it, Tania, can you go with him? I think Madame Arcati could have some quite entertaining business with a shawl, and I believe there's rather an exotic Indian version somewhere in the costume store."

"We will head there immediately," said Tania, and she and Ron made their way down the back stairs which led to the wardrobe department, hidden away in the depths of the theatre beneath the front stalls.

On arrival, they were met with a gruff "Now what does she want?" from Dorothy, the wardrobe supervisor seated in her little cubbyhole by the entrance who, rumour had it, had been running the department with an iron fist since the days of Tania's grandmother, one of the original founders of the group. She was a tall lean woman, age impossible to guess, never seen wearing anything other than baggy jeans atop a tee shirt, and a cardigan festooned with safety pins. Despite her initial unprepossessing manner, she was universally regarded as mistress of her craft, and had a talent for producing the most perfect costumes for any given production on an unbelievably small budget. And an occasional twinkle in her eye, ruthlessly concealed from new members in the interests of discipline, but allowed to gleam forth with more well-established performers, was sometimes accompanied by a reluctant smile as she revealed her latest brilliant creation or find.

"Good evening, Dorothy!" Tania was not to be intimidated, and greeted the wardrobe supervisor cheerily. "Nothing too demanding, you'll be delighted to hear."

"I'm glad about that," grunted Dorothy.

"Leah wants my character to have a shawl for some business, and she says you may have something suitable amongst your bits and pieces. Indian, she says?"

It took only a moment's thought. "I've got just the thing." Dorothy stood and reached down a cardboard box perched on a precarious-looking shelf above her head, and after a few seconds' burrowing produced an impressive fringed shawl in an Indian design, peacock blue with intricately embroidered flowers in multi-coloured silks.

"That's marvellous," enthused Tania. "May I borrow it for rehearsal?"

"If you promise to look after it," replied Dorothy. "It's quite valuable."

"Word of honour," said Tania. "I hope you're managing to sort out all the play's costumes that quickly."

"Not so's you'd notice," said Dorothy. "Have you any idea how difficult it is to track down genuine bias-cut 1930s frocks in the right colours for Elvira and Ruth?"

"I'm sure it's a nightmare," sympathised Tania. "But we have every faith in your talents. I bet you've managed to source something suitable."

"Well, as a matter of fact, I have," admitted Dorothy reluctantly. "I've got a friend, Suzanne Heming, who's wardrobe mistress of the Westwick Players, and I've been to see her. We're going to borrow a couple of dresses from her stock."

"That's wonderful," smiled Tania. "Problem solved."

"Oh, Sooz is a great problem solver," said Dorothy. "She needs to be, in her job."

"Oh yes? What does she do?" enquired Ron.

"She's a forensic investigator with the police," declared Dorothy. "Very good too, I gather. In fact, she told me something very interesting when I saw her yesterday. It's about this man who died at the abbey the other day."

"Professor Langley?" Tania's interest was instantly piqued. "What was it that she found that was so interesting?"

"Aha!" said Dorothy. "So you're investigating that, are you? I might have known you had a taste for these things, after the Cornwall business. So you think it wasn't an accident?"

Tania shrugged. "I really don't know. There's no actual evidence to say so."

"Then you listen to this." Dorothy had now unbent completely. "According to Sooz, the body was sent to them for forensic examination, because it was an unexplained death. Well, unexplained in a way, although from what she said, the man had fallen head-first on to a stone floor, so that his head was an awful mess. But the thing was ..." She paused dramatically.

"Yes?"

"There weren't any injuries to the man's arms. No broken bones. No smashed hands. And that's what she's put in her report."

"I don't see what that has to do with anything," said a puzzled Ron.

"I think I do," said Tania, suddenly excited. "Think of it, Ron. If you'd toppled over that balcony in the abbey when you almost overbalanced the other day, you'd instinctively put your arms out in front of you as you fell to try to cushion the fall somehow. Now obviously, from that height, it wouldn't do a bit of good, but that's what you'd do. But it sounds as if the professor didn't. He landed smack on his head. So surely that must mean one thing."

"And what's that?"

"He was already dead when he went over the edge. And that definitely makes it murder!"

*

At that moment, Susannah popped her head round the door of the wardrobe department. "Oh, you are still here. Leah says we're just about to start the next scene."

"No tea for us then," said Ron. "We'd better get back upstairs. Oh, but just before we go, Dorothy, Leah wants me in a jacket. It doesn't matter what sort for rehearsal, as long as there's a side pocket I can tuck my hand in. Do you think you could sort me one out?"

"Leave it with me," said Dorothy. "I've got your measurements in my little book. I'll get the new girl to find you one."

"New girl?" queried Ron.

"Can't stop now. It doesn't do to keep Leah waiting. We'll pop back at the end of rehearsal," said Tania, and pushed Ron towards the door.

*

"Thank you, ladies and gentlemen. See you at the next rehearsal."

As Leah dismissed the company amid a flurry of 'Goodbyes' and 'Anyone else coming to the pub?', Tania caught hold of Ron's arm. "I'd better take this shawl back down to Dorothy," she said. "I don't want to be in her bad books for unauthorised removal of part of her costume stock. You know she gets tetchy if people just swan in and borrow things."

The couple descended to Dorothy's domain, to find the wardrobe mistress still ensconced in her cubbyhole, a needle and thread in her hand as she attended to a small repair on a beaded dress.

"Here's that shawl back," said Tania. "It was perfect, so may I borrow it for rehearsals in future?"

"You may," said Dorothy. "And while you're here, Ron, you may as well try on that jacket you wanted. I'll get the new girl to bring it through." She leaned out of the doorway and called, "Jennifer! Bring that jacket out, would you?"

There was movement among the racks of hanging costumes, and a familiar face appeared.

"Jenny!" exclaimed Tania in surprise. "What on earth are you doing here?"

"This is my new wardrobe assistant," explained Dorothy. "So do you two know each other?"

"Jenny works for me part-time in the library," replied Tania. "But I didn't know she was involved here as well."

"I've only just started," said Jenny. "I saw the notice on the board at the library asking for new members to join R.O.A.D.S. to help out backstage, and you're always going on about the plays and such at work, so I thought it would be fun. It would give me something to do in the evenings. So here I am."

"Well," laughed Ron, "welcome aboard. I'm sure Dorothy will be glad of the help. It can't be easy running this part of the ship single-handed. Now, about this jacket ..."

As Ron slipped his arms into the coat, Jenny drew Tania aside. "I'm so glad you're here. Now I don't have to wait until tomorrow to tell you," she gushed breathlessly.

"Tell me what?"

"I couldn't stop thinking about that man who's died at the abbey," began Jenny, "so I've been doing some research on the internet. And you'll never guess what I've discovered."

"I have a feeling this is going to be a long story," smiled Tania. "Why don't we adjourn to the pub and you can tell us all about it?" And as Ron handed back the jacket to Dorothy with a nod of thanks and a brief 'That'll be just right', the couple and Jenny made their way out of the theatre and across the road to the Pilgrim's Rest.

Comfortably settled in a quiet corner away from the hubbub of R.O.A.D.S. players clustered at the bar, Tania looked expectantly at Jenny. "Well?"

"There's a legend about Saint Elfleda," began the young woman. "It was already going about in mediaeval times, according to the site I found, and it's called 'The Saint and the Demon'."

"Sounds intriguing," remarked Ron.

"You wait till you hear it. You see, they said that Saint Elfleda had just finished building her new abbey church, and it was just about to be consecrated, but then a horrible black demon flew down and perched on the roof, and all the local priests were called in, and even the Bishop of Westchester, but nothing they could do could get rid of it. They tried everything – holy water, excommunication, and goodness knows what. But then Elfleda called all her nuns together and they all prayed for a day and a night, and because of their great purity, the demon was defeated. But here's the best bit."

"Go on," urged Tania.

"The story tells that the demon was cast down from a great height, and that he fell to the ground and was smashed into pieces. There!" concluded Jenny triumphantly.

"As was Professor Langley," murmured Tania, half to herself.

"That's just like the picture in the Book of Hours, love," pointed out Ron. "Don't you remember? That devil perched on the church. We saw it when we went up to the museum to look at it, before any of this happened. And now that we know it's actually murder, from what Dorothy's friend told her, could it possibly be that the professor's killing was inspired by a mediaeval manuscript?"

"You don't think it could have been Elfleda herself who ...?" Jenny gazed at the couple, open-mouthed, eyes wide with speculation.

"Of course not!" retorted Tania robustly. "Don't be ridiculous. It couldn't be." She reflected for a moment. "Could it ...?"

Chapter 13
Saturday

Tania sat bolt upright in bed. "I'm an idiot!"

The alarm radio had only just turned on, with its menu of light classical music designed to ease listeners gently into the day, and Ron was still in the process of surfacing from deep slumber. "Don't be too hard on yourself, love," he murmured sleepily. "Everyone knows you can't fight nature."

Tania reacted with a swipe to the recumbent form alongside her which was only just on the right side of the borderline between playful and effective. "What is it we haven't done?" she demanded.

"I don't know. Woken up properly?"

Tania sighed. "Examined the scene of the crime, of course. Which we're now sure it is. Who's to say there may not be something that's so glaringly obvious that everyone else has overlooked it?"

"Certainly not me, love," said Ron, propping himself up and smiling blearily at his wife. "So, is the plan to leap forth and rush immediately to the abbey to take a look at ... what is it they call it ... the *locus in quo*?"

Tania gave a gentle laugh. "Oh, all right," she conceded. "Perhaps not immediately."

"So there's still time for a cup of tea?" enquired Ron. He stretched, swivelled round to put his feet to the floor, and reached for his dressing-gown. "I'd better get up and make one then."

*

"You realise we'll need to get our skates on," pointed out Ron, as he closed the front door behind the couple. "At least, you will. If you haven't got the library doors open at the stroke of eleven o'clock, the pavement outside will be thronged with middle-aged ladies in woolly hats and cardigans battering on the woodwork because they're desperate for their weekly fix of Cookson or Cooper."

"That is a dreadful calumny on our clientele," protested Tania with mock indignation. "There are plenty of middle-aged men in cardigans as well." She gave a chuckle. "And I might draw your attention to the fact that one of my most prominent borrowers is an eighty-seven-year-old

woman who is studying for a masters in nuclear physics at the Open University, so you can stick your clichés somewhere appropriately un-sunny!"

"Oops!" replied Ron. "My mistake, love. But it doesn't detract from my point. Time is limited."

"So less talking, more driving," said Tania, as the car pulled out into the street. "Anyway, I've thought it all through. Now I grant you, it wouldn't really have been the done thing to sneak into the abbey for the early service, because the rector might have taken a rather dim view if we'd gone peering about the place on the lookout for clues, instead of sitting quietly like respectful attendees in the pews. However, the abbey opens its doors to visitors at nine-thirty on a Saturday, so ..." She checked her watch. "... if you park in the free two-hour zone a couple of streets away ..."

"Because we'll never get a spot on the Market Square with all the stalls taking up the space," put in Ron.

"Then we should be able to arrive just as Peter is opening up the Jerusalem Porch. Which will give us an hour and twenty-five minutes to take a look around, and five minutes for me to sprint across the square and open up for the afore-mentioned cardiganned brigade."

"Planned with military precision," grinned Ron appreciatively. "Now, let's see if somebody has very kindly left us a parking hole along here."

As the couple approached the Jerusalem Porch, they were just in time to see Peter Hawkley placing the customary sandwich board outside the entrance announcing the opening of the building. "Good morning, Peter," Tania hailed him cheerfully. "I see we managed to time that well."

"Goodness," replied Peter. "You two are eager. I normally get a few moments to draw breath before the public start to turn up."

"Oh, don't think of us as the public," smiled Tania. "We're just friends of the abbey coming to take a little look around at a couple of things. But I expect we're probably the first people in today."

"Actually, no," said Peter. "Most of the abbey team have beaten you to it this morning. We've got quite a busy day, what with a school party coming to visit this morning. Nine-year-olds."

"A school party?" Ron's eyebrows rose. "You'll have your work cut out with them!"

"Not at all," smiled Peter. "Taking children around is one of my favourite parts of the job. Wouldn't be without it. They absolutely love it, once I get going. For a start, there's the fact that they're walking over dozens of buried bodies, which always makes the girls squeal, and then we've got a crusader knight whose heart was removed so that it could be buried in Jerusalem, and everybody goes 'Ugh!', not to mention the mediaeval countess who was locked up by King John in Westchester Castle and gnawed to death by rats. Children love tales of death and horror. And I always finish up with a visit to the crypt for a few extra bodies, followed by a walk along the secret passage to look for ghosts."

"Secret passage?" echoed Tania. "I didn't know there was one."

"There isn't really," said Peter. "It's just a passageway that runs underneath the nave from the crypt beneath the altar and the chancel along to the chamber at the bottom of the tower spiral stairs. Most people don't even know it's there, and the crypt entrance is hidden behind one of the tombs. I don't know what the nuns used it for, but it's quite dark and spidery, so it's quite a good way to finish the children's tour on a fun note."

"Sounds as if you'll be up to your ears," said Ron.

"Not just me. We've got a wedding this afternoon, so pretty much everyone is already hard at it. I believe Sharon's already busy knocking up extra batches of her sticky buns for the children, and Louise has got her ladies making a start on the flower arrangements, and I shouldn't be at all surprised if Heather is doing a special display of her Elfleda teddy bears to tempt a few of the kids to part with their pocket money."

"Sounds like a hive of activity," remarked Ron. "We'll do our best to keep out of everybody's way. We just planned to pop up to the museum to ... have another look around."

"Oh." Peter sounded surprised. "Any special reason?"

"No, not particularly," Ron replied in reassuring tones. "It's just that Tania had a couple of thoughts that she wanted to check out." He jumped slightly as the Jerusalem Porch door crashed closed behind him, as an anorak-clad couple wielding Nordic walking sticks made their way into the entrance. "And you evidently have customers, so we'll let you get on with it." With a farewell smile, he took Tania by the arm, and the couple made their way into the nave of the church. "So now what?"

"Straight up to the museum, I think," said Tania.

"I should think so. That little chat with Peter has already soaked up several of your precious minutes," observed Ron. "Right, let's get on with it."

But their best intentions went almost immediately astray as, approaching the space below the museum parapet, they encountered Louise Froyle with a cushion of white chrysanthemums in her hands, in the process of positioning it on the floor.

"Oh, that's pretty, Louise," remarked Tania. "Is that part of your arrangements for today's wedding?" A thought struck her. "Or is it some sort of tribute to the late Professor Langley?"

"Hmph," retorted Louise gruffly. "A bit of both, I suppose. Although I wouldn't exactly call it a tribute. After the way that man went on to the people here, I'm not sure that there'll be that many tears shed for him. But he's dead, and it doesn't do to be uncharitable."

"Well, I think it's rather tasteful," said Tania. "And kind."

"Kind hasn't got anything to do with it," replied Louise. "Look at this." She moved the flowers aside, to reveal a patch of discolouration on the flagstones beneath.

Ron peered. "Is that ... blood?" he enquired.

"Blood, and goodness-knows-what besides," said Louise. "Best not to think about it too hard. It's where the professor hit the ground head-first, so it made quite a mess. But the trouble is, we've tried to wash it away, but the stain has seeped into the stone. And by now I'm sure everybody knows all about what happened here, even if they're not sure exactly where, and the last thing today's bride needs is to be wading through pools of blood on her way to the altar. So I thought the best thing was to make up this little arrangement to disguise the spot."

"And I'm sure nobody will give it a second's thought," said Tania. "So well done." She exchanged glances with her husband. "And I'm certain you've got loads to get on with, so we won't keep you. Come on, Ron." She headed for the lift.

"So where do you want to start?" wondered Ron as the pair emerged on the museum level.

Tania shook her head. "I don't really know," she

confessed. "But I'm sure there must be something."

"You reckon the police have missed something that's so obvious that it's going to jump out at us, amateurs that we are? Don't forget that, according to what we know, the forensic people have already been up here to survey the scene, and it doesn't look as if they found anything worth noting," Ron reminded her.

"Ah," countered Tania, "but they weren't necessarily examining it as a crime scene. They didn't yet know, from what Dorothy's friend let slip, that the professor didn't seem to have made any effort to save himself when he went over the edge. It's only during the post-mortem that they found that out, so they're bound to come to the same conclusion as me."

"That he was dead when he went over?"

"Exactly. I think we can surely rule out the possibility that someone simply gave him a push."

"Even though that parapet's pretty low? It wouldn't have taken much effort. Almost anyone could have done it if they'd taken him by surprise."

"Yes, but he wouldn't have gone over in complete silence," insisted Tania. "He'd have cried out, and nobody's reported hearing anything like a yell. No, the only thing that makes sense to me is that he was already dead when he hit the floor."

"Okay," conceded Ron. "So how was he killed? Again, by the sound of it, there weren't any wounds to the body, or else forensics would have picked them up. But the head's a different matter."

"Agreed."

"Rather too much matter, if that stain downstairs is anything to go by," grimaced Ron. "So what are the options? He could have been shot." He reflected briefly. "No, that's not possible, surely, because somebody would have heard it if a gun went off. You know how this place echoes. And I'm having trouble imagining some sort of professional assassin equipped with a gun with a silencer. I know that the professor doesn't sound like the sort of person it's easy to get on with, and it seems as if he was capable of expressing some pretty harsh opinions, but I can't think that even the most violent disagreements in the academic atmosphere at Camford would lead to that sort of outcome."

"I think you may have been watching too much Inspector Morse," smiled Tania.

"Just thinking out loud, love," replied Ron, a touch defensively. "So, carrying on, we need a nice silent weapon. What's quieter than a nice dagger?"

"I'm not sure that the religious paraphernalia in this museum runs to daggers," pointed out Tania. "I mean, we can check, but I doubt it. Unless we now have the image of some ecclesiastical loyalist, a fervent admirer of Saint Elfleda, creeping stealthily up behind the professor, stiletto in hand, intent on wreaking revenge for the slight to the saint?"

"Now you're being silly," huffed Ron. "But seriously, there's nothing to say that this was premeditated. Isn't it perfectly possible that there's something around here that could have been used to stab Langley before tipping him over the edge?" A thought suddenly struck him. "Something like the scissors Louise uses when she's trimming the flowers for her arrangements."

"You're surely not suggesting that it was Louise who was responsible?" protested Tania. "Don't forget, she was the one who first came across the body, and according to Sharon, she was shaken to the roots. I mean, I know the cliché in loads of murder mysteries is that the first person to find a dead body is often the last one to see them alive, but even so ..." She shook her head in disbelief.

"No, of course I'm not accusing Louise," retorted

Ron. "But don't you remember? When we were down talking to her, just as we were about to leave, she was muttering on about her pair of gardening gloves having gone missing. If you were purloining her scissors to stab somebody, what would be more sensible than to use the gloves sitting there to avoid getting your fingerprints on the murder weapon?"

"Which would make the murder premeditated," observed Tania. "And as you say, we have no reason to suppose that it was. Or that the professor was stabbed in the first place."

"Shame that the head was such a mess," mused Ron. "Maybe it will never be possible to tell exactly what killed him." His eyes lit up. "Do you know, we're fools. What have we forgotten?"

"I don't know. What?"

"The good old traditional blunt instrument," declared Ron triumphantly. "What better than a good solid whack on the head to kill somebody, especially if they are then going to very helpfully smack down head-first on a nice stone floor, thereby obliterating any evidence of the blow?"

Tania sighed in irritation. "Of course! As I think I may have mentioned first thing this morning, I am an idiot. So, the question is, what could have been used to deliver said blow?"

Ron looked around. "Well, there are plenty of candidates around here, as far as I can see. So let's take a look."

"We'd better be quick," said Tania. "I wouldn't mind betting that Dorothy's friend's conclusions have come to the attention of the police detectives by now, so you can bet that the forensics people will be all over this place before you can say 'knife'."

"Or, in this case, 'blunt instrument'," quipped Ron. "But I think you're right. And wouldn't it be nice if we could present them with something before we get thrown out of here as a closed crime scene, which you can bet we will be."

"Then don't just stand there. Look."

The couple split up and began to range around the exhibits dotted about the museum on their display stands and shelves. "There's a lumpy old crosier here," suggested Ron. "That could have done some damage."

"Too unwieldy," replied Tania. "It's six feet long. You'd never sneak up on someone with that. But what about a Victorian police truncheon? That's easier to handle, and it's pretty solid."

"Any sign that it's been used?"

Tania looked closely at the item. "No," she admitted reluctantly. "Clean as a whistle. How about one of these silver chalices? They're quite sturdy."

"Yes, but they're locked up in their cabinet. You'd have quite a fiddle unlocking it to get at them. Somebody might get suspicious."

"Drat!"

"There's a fine selection of little stone statuettes here," said Ron. "They probably used to stand in little niches in the various chapels. Shame that they've all had their heads knocked off." He pulled a face. "Rather like the late unlamented professor. But you could certainly pick one of these up and swing it to some effect." He demonstrated.

"And not too heavy for anyone to use," added Tania. "And there ought to be some sort of marks on it, if that stain in the stones downstairs is anything to go by. Any traces?"

Ron gave the figures a swift examination. "Nothing that I can see."

"We're running out of candidates," said Tania with a sigh. She looked along the final display case, until her eye fell on the museum's former prize exhibit, displaced in favour of Saint Elfleda's Book of Hours. The colours on the intricately-carved stone boss hinted at the splendour of the original when it was in place in the Earl's mortuary chapel. But there was one part of the colour scheme which did not seem to sit well with its fellows. One edge bore an irregular stain, coloured a rusty red. "Ron," she said in strained tones.

"What's up, love?"

"Come and take a look at this."

Her husband moved to her side and peered closely at the indicated area. The pair exchanged glances.

"I think you're right," said Ron. "We've found it."

"And that proves it," said Tania. "Professor Langley was killed by the boss."

*

"I hope that's not a formal accusation against the Rector of Ramston Abbey."

The pair whirled around at the voice which spoke unexpectedly behind them.

"Goodness!" exclaimed Tania. "You made me jump. I didn't know anyone was there."

"Apologies for that, madam," said the man who had spoken. He looked to be in his late thirties, with a stocky frame a little above medium height and a friendly face topped by a semi-tamed mop of tousled hair. "But I'd be interested to know why you made the remark you just did."

"Well," replied Tania, slightly flustered, "somebody has died here, and everyone seemed to think it was an accident, but then we heard something which didn't quite fit, so we came up here to see if we could find any evidence."

"Evidence?" echoed the man. "That's an interesting choice of words, madam. I'm wondering why you chose it. And I'd also be interested to know exactly who you are, and why you're here."

"I'm Tania Faye, and this is my husband Ron. We live in Ramston. And we were just ... intrigued by the whole mystery, because it sounded like a murder."

The man's face creased in a slow smile. "Ah. Light begins to dawn. And perhaps I'd better introduce myself." He reached into a jacket pocket to produce a wallet, whose contents he displayed to the couple. "My warrant card. I'm Detective Inspector Copper, and this ..." He indicated the slightly younger, and slightly chubbier, curly-headed man standing one step behind and below him on the spiral stair. "... is my colleague Detective Sergeant Radley. And there's been a tale going about the station of a woman from around this neck of the woods who recently caused our colleagues in the Cornwall Constabulary a touch of embarrassment by beating them to the solution of a murder down there. We all enjoyed a few quiet smiles at the story. I don't suppose that, by any remote chance, that woman would be you, would it?"

"Guilty as charged, inspector," admitted Ron cheerfully. "Tania put all the clues together and figured it out brilliantly."

"I see," said the inspector drily. "So you thought you might try your hand at doing the same here?"

"Only because of what we heard about the report of Professor Langley's injuries," explained Tania. "They didn't sound right, if it was an accident."

"And how did this information come your way?" demanded Copper sternly.

"Oh. Um. It was ... I think it was a friend of a friend," faltered Tania. "I can't quite remember exactly."

"Hmmm," said the inspector, with a frown. "Sergeant, remind me to have a little chat with the Forensics team about discretion and security," he remarked over his shoulder to his colleague. "Especially their senior officer."

"Oops! Someone's going to be in hot water when

you get home tonight," the sergeant could be heard to murmur.

Copper turned back to Tania. "So, reverting to your original remark about the death of Professor Langley. Can you explain exactly what you meant."

Tania drew a deep breath. "Well, because of ... what we heard ... it sounded as if the professor must have been already dead when he landed on the floor below the parapet here. So someone must have killed him up here, by some means or another, and we were looking around to see how that might have been done, and ... I just saw this." She indicated the carved piece of stonework. "It's a boss from the ceiling of one of the abbey's chapels. It's one of the museum's prize exhibits because of the surviving mediaeval paintwork, except ... well, what's there now isn't all paint. Take a look."

The inspector stepped forward, the sergeant at his side, and examined the stone boss closely. "Radley," he commanded briskly. "Get on the phone. I want Forensics back here double-quick, and I want this area sealed off immediately as a crime scene."

"Will do, sir." The sergeant stepped aside and began to murmur into his phone.

"And you, Mr and Mrs Faye," continued Copper, "had better come with me." He started down the spiral stairs.

Chapter 14
Saturday

Reaching the back of the nave, the inspector led the way towards the rearmost of the pews and indicated to Tania and Ron that they should take a seat, while he remained standing, regarding them with brows drawn into a slight frown.

"So you think it is murder then, inspector?" ventured Tania.

Copper let out a quiet sigh. "I'm prepared to consider it a suspicious death, yes. But that is all I'm prepared to say for the moment." His voice grew stern. "But, Mrs Faye, grateful as I am for the fact that you've drawn my attention to something that ought not to have been missed during an earlier examination of the scene by my forensic colleagues ..." He paused, apparently combating some inner irritation which Tania could not quite fathom. "... that does not mean that I am prepared for your involvement in this matter to go any further than that. I do not, repeat not, want you to have any thoughts about replicating your amateur sleuthing activities in Cornwall. Leave this to the professionals. I hope I make myself clear?"

"Oh, completely, inspector," responded Tania, with such unaccustomed meekness that Ron could not help giving his wife a quizzical sideways look.

"I have just one question for you both. Professor Langley's death occurred on Wednesday. Was either of you in the abbey then?"

"Absolutely not, inspector," declared Ron. "We were nowhere near." He reflected for a moment. "Although, thinking about it, actually yes. We were. But not at the time."

"Well, which was it?" enquired Copper with a touch of asperity. "Were you here or not?"

"We were here earlier in the day," explained Tania. "You see, there had been a discovery of an old manuscript here which sounded rather interesting, so we came over to the museum to take a look. I'm chief librarian at the town's library across the square, you see, and there's always the chance that I'm going to be asked about anything to do with Ramston's history, so I like to keep abreast. But that's all. We weren't here during the evening when the professor ... well, you know ... when whatever happened, happened."

"I see," said the inspector. "And was either of you acquainted with Professor Langley?"

"Not at all," replied Ron. "Never met him."

"He was quite a prominent academic at Camford University, I believe, so I think I'd possibly heard of him in passing," added Tania.

"And we certainly heard a lot about him after he'd passed," said Ron, to receive a sharp dig in the ribs from his wife.

The inspector pounced on the remark. "Oh? In what way?"

"Oh, just that everyone was saying what a terrible thing it was that he'd died," said Tania airily. "You must know what small towns are like, inspector. There's always a lot of talk."

"Hmmm." Copper looked at the couple askance, evidently not wholly convinced by Tania's explanation. "But in that case, Mr and Mrs Faye, I don't see any reason to keep you any longer, so I will leave you to carry on with your day. But," he warned, gazing steadily at the pair with stern emphasis, "please remember that, as of now, your involvement with this matter is at an end. I do not expect our paths to cross again. Understood?"

"With crystal clarity, inspector," responded Tania with a sweet smile. "And I'd better hurry, or I shall be late for work. Let's leave the inspector to do his job, Ron." She linked arms with her husband, and the two made for the Jerusalem Porch.

*

"Well, that's us told," remarked Ron, as the couple hurried across the Market Square in the direction of the library. "You're just going to have to leave the whole thing alone until the police come up with some answers."

Tania let out a merry tinkling laugh. "You think?" She halted and extended a hand towards her husband. "How do you do? I don't think we've met. My name's Tania Faye."

"What on earth are you on about, woman?" enquired a bewildered Ron.

"Oh Ron, you surely don't think I'm going to leave it there, do you?" smiled his wife. "Not when we know so much about what went on before the professor died. There's a whole lot of people who had good reasons to wish him ill, and there's probably no way that the police can get anywhere near what we already know. So if Inspector Copper thinks I'm going to give up, he's got another think coming. For a start, I'm going to make a list of our suspects, and then we'll see about having a talk with each of them to see what we can find out."

"And how do you propose to do that without treading on the police's feet?" protested Ron. "And don't forget, love, you've got a library to run as well. Starting in ..." He checked his watch. "... exactly six minutes."

"Just you leave it to me," said Tania, fumbling in her handbag for the keys to the library's front door. "I'm a resourceful woman. I'll get on with my side of things. And didn't you mention yesterday that the grass at the back of the house needed a trim? And I thought we might have a lamb casserole tonight, and you know that nobody makes it like you."

"Dismissed to domestic duties," grinned Ron wryly. "The curse of the house-husband. Very well then, you carry on with what the inspector calls your amateur sleuthing, but don't complain to me if it gets you into hot water with him, Miss Marple. Or do you prefer 'Jessica Fletcher'?"

"Cheek! Do you realise how old Angela Lansbury was when she played that part?" returned Tania. "Now go away, and we'll both get on with what each of us does best." With a fond peck on her husband's lips, she unlocked the library and disappeared inside.

*

"That, darling, was one of your best," declared Tania, laying down her knife and fork and taking a sip of wine. "I did point out that you have an unrivalled touch when it comes to lamb casserole, did I not?"

"You did, love," smiled a gratified Ron. "But then, my old ma did pass on a few of her skills to me when it came to making a nice bit of stew."

"Don't do yourself down," laughed Tania. "You have other talents." And hastily, as Ron raised a quirky hopeful eyebrow in her direction, "Culinary, that is!" She feigned a frown of disapproval as her husband adopted an expression of thwarted expectation. "Bad man! So what does the chef propose for dessert this evening?"

"I thought an Eton Mess would go down rather nicely," said Ron. "Followed by a cup of that Blue Mountain coffee we haven't got around to trying yet. And then, finally, you can tell me what you've been up to today."

On her return from work, Tania had steadfastly refused to reveal what further steps she had made with regard to her plans for investigating Tarquin Langley's death.

"No," she had stated forthrightly. "We've been concentrating on nothing other than this murder for days. Aside from that, I've had a very hectic day at the library, with some very silly people asking some very inane questions, to which I have to reply with my most professional smile, even if it is sometimes through gritted teeth. But even so, I've managed to make some progress, which I will tell you about later. But I thought we ought to have some time this evening to be just an ordinary married couple, before we get back into the question of murder and mayhem. And I'm going to start off by having a long slow soak in the bath."

Ron had gathered his wife into a hug. "Good plan, love. Give your brain a chance to recharge. And with that in mind, I will go and start it running for you with some of those lavender bubbles you like, and then I will scare up as many candles from around the house as I can to help create a nice soothing ambience. I may even nip out to the garden and harvest a few rose petals to scatter on the water."

"You, my darling, are a romantic fool," chuckled Tania.

"Oh, I can do better than that," said Ron. "I'll get the loungers out on the patio and whip up a jug of cocktails. We can sit out there sipping Margaritas and inhaling the smell of newly-mown grass until it's time for dinner. Will that suit your ladyship?"

"What have I done to deserve you?" murmured Tania as she snuggled in to her husband.

"I can think of many things," replied Ron. "So please, just keep doing them." He broke from the embrace. "And this, to repeat the wise words of my old granny, isn't going to get the babby washed, so leave go of me, woman. I've got a date with a hot tap." He headed up the stairs in the direction of the bathroom.

*

Seated in the living room in the aftermath of the meal, the aroma of freshly-brewed coffee rising from the cups in front of them, Ron regarded his wife expectantly. "Well?" he enquired. "Is the game afoot?"

"It is," responded Tania. "And the first thing I did, in amongst the general aggravations of this afternoon, was to compile a list of those people who could have had it in for Tarquin Langley."

"I thought we already had a pretty clear idea of who that might be," queried Ron.

"Darling," pointed out Tania, "you married a librarian. We have a passion for order and method. And lists. So, we already know the 'how'. I'm betting that what looked like a bloodstain on the stone boss will turn out to be exactly that, once Inspector Copper has given his forensic people a good talking-to, so there's our murder weapon. And we've got the 'who', together with as much as we have so far as to the 'why'. Although there may well be more on that front."

"Good thought. So, fire away. Although," Ron mused, "you could always have tried to channel your inner Madame Arcati and attempted to communicate with the spirit of the departed in order to discover who gave him that whack."

Tania, after giving her husband a look, produced a notebook. "As I was saying ..."

"That looks suspiciously like library issue," remarked Ron. "Isn't that regarded in some quarters as theft from your employer?" He quailed under Tania's stern glance. "Sorry, love. Just thinking we'd better make sure we stay on the right side of the law."

"To begin with," resumed Tania with dignity, "I have identified those people who were in the abbey at the time of the incident, and are therefore suspects. And ridiculous as it may appear, we can't exclude Cassandra Milton."

"I think you're right. She and the professor evidently had history going back quite some way, although how you're going to winkle out the possibly unsavoury details in casual conversation beats me."

"Not only that, but the rector seems to have been fierce in defending the abbey against any attempt by Langley to deprive it of its newest treasure."

"Like a mother defending her young?" suggested Ron. "Some animals will go to extremes. Maybe the same extends to clergywomen." He shrugged. "So, moving on ..."

"And another person with history with the professor, no pun intended, is Rudolph Wheatley. I get the impression that the two may have been locking horns in the groves of academe over a period of years. Now that's probably not unusual in university circles – you've only got to watch Morse or Lewis to see the results of all manner of scholastic rivalries. But whether this business of Saint Elfleda's manuscript could have brought things to a violent head ..."

"Again, presumably no pun intended," muttered Ron under his breath.

"... is another matter. Defence of Rudolph's own reputation and of the abbey might have combined to provide a powerful cocktail."

"Couldn't the same argument apply to Peter Hawkley?" enquired Ron. "Presumably he's on your list too."

"He is," nodded Tania. "Unlikely as he may seem. He's such a lovely man, and it's hard to imagine him doing anything which might harm the abbey in the eyes of the world. He does love the place so much. But again, that might be a reason for him to wish the professor ill. But he'd only just met Langley for the first time. Is it really plausible to decide to murder a man you've never met before?"

"Don't they always say that the good thing about taking an instant dislike to somebody is that it saves time later?" quipped Ron. "And to counter your argument, it doesn't sound as if the professor was holding back on his opinions of Peter, according to what Louise overheard."

"True," agreed Tania.

"And on the subject of unflattering opinions as expressed by the professor, surely Heather Clanville has to be in the frame. Yes ..." Ron held up a hand as if to forestall any protest by his wife. "Heather's surely not your identikit murderer. And she was reportedly in something of a state in the aftermath of Langley's death. Now whether that was just the shock of the event, or the result of what Sharon heard him say about her shop, we can't offhand tell. Maybe remarks about mothers and their young apply here as well. And if the shop's reputation and value to the abbey got trashed, then that's Heather left out in the cold."

"I know," sighed Tania. "Which is why she's listed along with the others. She was, after all, on the premises at the crucial time. But as for motivation, you might as well suggest that Sharon Burley could have had it in for the professor because he took against her baking."

"Which, in my humble opinion, is probably a capital offence in itself," grinned Ron. "And if the man had been struck with a rock cake instead of a rock, you could probably make a sound case against her."

"Let's not get silly," replied Tania.

"So is that everyone?" queried Ron.

"Well, yes and no. You see, Adrian Hinton was up in the organ loft around the right time, but there's no link between him and the professor, and I don't see how he could have got to the museum undetected. On the other hand, we've got a couple of people who were involved in clashes with Langley, and although they seem to have left the abbey before the time of his death, there's nothing to say that they didn't return for one final moment of conflict."

"I assume you're talking about Pandora Weston and Robin Barton."

"Absolutely. If you're talking about reputations being trashed, then Langley seems to have had quite a thing against Pandora and her Sister Cat novels. I can't think why he should be so against them," mused Tania, "unless he thought that in some way they demeaned his field of academic activity. But for Pandora, it sounds as if he was nothing less than gratuitously offensive. And if I know anything at all about writers ..."

"Which you surely do, having come across a few in your career," put in Ron.

"... they are never going to take kindly to somebody attempting to destroy something they've put their heart and soul into."

"And then we come on to Robin," said Ron. "Which in some ways gives the most obvious motivation. Langley propositioned him, with menaces. There are two ways to deal with that. Either you ignore the threat and try to ride out any resulting storm, or else you might decide to take drastic action to nip the situation in the bud. Could you see him doing that? You know him somewhat. I don't."

"I've only met him in the library when he's come in with Tom," replied Tania. "But the one strong impression I get is that the pair of them are totally wrapped up in one another. So if anything were to threaten that, who knows what a person might do?"

"And that seems to be your list," said Ron. "That is, unless we've got some random late-night visitors to the abbey with a grudge against Tarquin Langley that we know nothing about."

Tania gave a small wince. "That's quite enough to be going on with, I think."

"So where do we go from here? You said the thing is to talk to all these people, while trying to keep out of the way of the police so as not to bring the inspector's wrath down upon our heads. And as it's Sunday tomorrow, it's not the best day to go traipsing around the abbey quizzing people."

"Ah," retorted Tania. "That is where I have been just a little crafty, I think. Because there are times when being the head librarian of Ramston has its uses."

"Go on," said Ron, intrigued.

"Word has come my way that Pandora is very close to finishing a new novel. I hear talk of a national tour of bookshops. So what would be more natural than to invite Pandora, Ramston's celebrity author, to come and give a talk at her local library? She's done it before. Of course, I would have to arrange a meeting with her to discuss the possibility. And who knows what other topics might arise during that conversation?"

"You, love, are an extremely cunning woman," said Ron admiringly. "And when might such a meeting take place?"

"Eleven-thirty tomorrow morning," responded Tania triumphantly. "As arranged over the phone today. We are invited for morning coffee."

Ron burst out laughing. "Cunning doesn't begin to cut it. I wish I were wearing a hat so that I could take it off to you."

"And then, of course, there's Rudolph Wheatley," said Tania, a twinkle in her eye.

"Go on," replied Ron in tones of mock resignation. "Astonish me."

"Afternoon tea tomorrow at five o'clock," laughed Tania.

"Another talk at the library?" hazarded Ron, eyebrows raised.

"Naturally. The citizens of the town have always been interested in its history, and what could be more compelling than the tale of the latest discovery at the abbey from the building's own historian? We shall pack the place with fascinated listeners, but of course I need to discuss the exact arrangements." Tania sat back, with a vain effort not to look too self-satisfied. "And as for everyone else, we'll busk it once we get into next week"

"I am proud of you, love," said Ron, heaving himself to his feet. He deposited a kiss on his wife's brow. "Now, what would you say to another cup of coffee? And maybe a nightcap to go with it? I believe we have rather a good bottle of brandy in the cupboard. That'll put us both in the mood for a nice relaxing night's sleep."

"Or ... not?" Tania's eyes sparkled as she regarded her husband with a smile.

Ron grinned. "Honestly! And you have the cheek sometimes to accuse me ..." He huffed in feigned disapproval. "I'd better get the glasses then," he said, and disappeared into the kitchen at speed.

Chapter 15
Sunday

"Tania, darling! Do come in!" Pandora Weston stepped back and, with a sweeping gesture, invited her visitors into her house. The couple stepped forward into the terraced cottage's diminutive living room, its walls dotted with a mixture of framed reproductions of the covers of Pandora's novels and eighteenth-century prints portraying pairs of romantic lovers in silken court costumes lounging in pastoral landscapes. One wall was occupied by a bookshelf whose contents ranged from leather-bound Victorian novelettes and brightly-coloured modern paperbacks to gleaming Palais-Royal caskets and plinth-mounted awards from publishing organisations. Pandora gestured her visitors towards a spindly-looking Regency two-seater sofa, while she cast herself into an ornate French fauteuil upholstered in a rich gold brocade.

"This is my husband Ron," said Tania.

"Nice to meet you, Miss Weston." Ron leaned forward and extended a hand.

"Pandora, please," insisted the novelist, keeping a lingering hold of the hand. She cast an appreciative eye over Tania's companion. "Well, Tania darling," she said, eyebrows raised. "Where have you been keeping this one? He's very good-looking, isn't he? Just the sort I like to use as a model for one of my romantic heroes. Not too muscular, good hair, and I'm sure I detect a hint of delightful danger in those eyes."

Ron blushed furiously. "I can hear you, you know," he protested. "And I'm not sure I agree with you about the danger bit."

Pandora leaned forward. "Trust me, Tania," she said conspiratorially. "I know what I'm talking about. I'd keep a tight hold on him if I were you."

"I intend to," smiled Tania, amused.

"Now," cried Pandora, suddenly leaping to her feet, "I promised you coffee, and coffee you shall have. Give me two minutes." She darted into what was evidently the kitchen at the back of the house, and very shortly there were sounds of whooshing and spluttering, before she returned with a tray bearing a gleaming silver coffee-pot, cream jug and sugar bowl, together with a trio of elegant bone china cups and saucers. "Do help yourselves," she said, placing the tray on the low table in the centre of the room. "I'm sure you know far better than I do how you like it. And then you can tell me what I can do for you."

"First of all, I'd like to thank you for sparing the time to see us," began Tania, once the coffees had been poured. "I'm sure you must be up to your ears in work."

"Always, darling," responded Pandora with a hint of tragic drama. "But for goodness' sake, don't apologise. The only thing you're taking me away from at the moment is proof-reading, which is one of the most exquisite forms of drudgery known to author-kind. But it has to be done, and to be honest, I don't trust anyone else to do it. Do you know – and I freely admit it was probably all my own fault for delegating – one of my books almost went to print with the hero being called both Luke and Lucian at different times. So now I take very great care. I couldn't bear to be laughed off the shelves, as it were."

"And I believe," ventured Tania, "that there's about to be a new Pandora Weston novel launched to the public."

"Yes, you mentioned that yesterday. You have some very good sources of information, darling," observed Pandora. "That's not supposed to be widely known until my publisher does a press release about the launch date."

"I need to keep myself informed about what

books are due to appear and when," explained Tania. "For stock-planning and purchasing. So I do have a few little birdies in the publishing business who tell me the occasional snippet."

"And you've heard one of these snippets about 'Rowena's Revenge', I gather."

"What a super title! And wouldn't it be marvellous if you could accompany the launch of your new novel with another of your popular talks at the library for your loyal home crowd?" coaxed Tania. "You know how well your talks have always gone in the past, and I wouldn't mind betting that the local press would cover it. Maybe even the nationals. And I can't imagine that your publishers would turn their nose up at the free publicity. It would leave more of their budget for paid promotion, and then we'd all be looking at another best-seller." Her face shone with enthusiasm.

Pandora thought for only a few seconds. "Darling," she said, "you're wonderfully persuasive. I think it would be churlish to refuse your kind offer. But just let me run it past my publisher, and I'll get back to you."

"Marvellous," smiled Tania. She finished her coffee and picked up her handbag as if to leave. "Oh, by the way," she added, guilelessly casual, "thinking even further ahead, I wonder whether the discovery of this new manuscript at the abbey might have provoked thoughts about a new book in your 'Sister Catherine' series?"

Pandora grew still for a moment, but then emitted a light laugh. "Heavens, darling," she said, waving a hand airily. "One thing at a time. I can't begin to contemplate another book before I've got this one launched out into the world."

"But wouldn't the topic be the perfect subject matter for one of Sister Cat's investigations?" persisted

Tania. "Mysterious goings-on at her abbey, with perhaps a dead body thrown in for good measure."

"A little like current events here in Ramston," added Ron, swiftly picking up his cue. "I expect you know all about it."

"I believe I did hear something about what's happened," admitted Pandora, a slight sense of strain detectable in her voice.

"Horrible, isn't it?" said Tania. "That poor Professor Langley. I wonder, did you know him?"

"No, not at all," declared Pandora hastily. "I'd never met him until ..." She bit the words off.

"Until what?" enquired Tania. "Oh, this sounds intriguing." She resumed her seat and gazed expectantly at Pandora. "Do tell."

"Well, as it happens, we did run into one another the other day," admitted the novelist reluctantly.

"At the abbey, was that? Or elsewhere? Because I believe he was supposed to be staying at the Cross Keys, wasn't he? I think that was what Dennis Dean said when we were chatting to him."

"Oh. I see." Pandora exuded an air of having been found out. "Well, actually, yes, the professor and I did exchange a few words when I dined in the hotel restaurant. Dennis mentioned my books, but I got the impression that the professor hadn't read any of them. But then after I'd eaten, I decided to pop over to the abbey to see their latest acquisition, because I'd had the same idea as you regarding a possible Sister Cat novel."

"Quite a coincidence," remarked Ron. "I expect it would have been very useful if the professor had been on hand to give you some information about the new manuscript. Shame he wasn't there."

"Actually, he did turn up later." Pandora was beginning to sound a touch flustered.

"What, in the abbey museum?"

"Yes. But we only spoke a little because he obviously had work to do, and as you know, I'm a slave to my proof-reading at the moment, so I couldn't spare too much time, and I came away."

"Not too late to be able to concentrate on your novel, I hope," sympathised Tania. "It can't be easy if you have to sit burning the candle long into the night."

"I suppose it must have been shortly before eight," replied Pandora.

"And Professor Langley was alive and well when you left?" asked Ron.

"Of course he was," snapped the novelist. "Why shouldn't he be?"

"Oh, no reason," said Tania lightly. "And you didn't return to the abbey after that? Nobody could have seen you?"

"Certainly not." Pandora began to sound exasperated, before a frown crossed her brow. "Why? Does somebody say they did?"

"Not to my knowledge. So that would have been the last time you saw the professor?"

"It was." Pandora's manner had changed from its former welcoming ease to a harder and chillier tone. "And I'm not at all sure why you should be so interested in the matter." She stood. "And now, if you will excuse me, I do have work to get on with. My publisher needs me to finish my read-through. And as for giving a talk at your library, Tania ..." She looked the librarian up and down. "Well, perhaps I'll call you. At some time."

*

"Whoa!" said Ron, as the couple stood once more on the pavement outside Pandora's front door. "She wasn't too fond of answering questions on the subject of Langley, was she?"

"Indeed not," agreed Tania. "And not only that. The answers she gave were, quite frankly, bare-faced lies."

"Which might lead us to think that she has something to hide."

"But necessarily murder?" demurred Tania. "Alright, she wasn't exactly candid when it came to describing her conversation with the professor in the pub restaurant, because I'm more inclined to believe Dennis's account than hers. On the other hand, there's wounded author's pride. Pandora's obviously totally invested in her books. And if Tarquin Langley was in danger of demolishing the potential subject matter of a new novel, that's another good reason for her to want him stopped."

"Except ..." mused Ron, "she left. She was gone from the abbey by the time the professor died. And we know this because of what Adrian Hinton told us. I can just picture her crashing out of the Jerusalem Porch like the wrath of god. Not only that, but there were other people queueing up to have a row with Langley after she'd departed. So does this mean that we have to rule her out?"

"I can't see that we can," said Tania. "Not with the motives we've got, together with the fact that she was wriggling on the hook just now. She could have lurked. The abbey's got plenty of dark corners."

"Which this isn't particularly," pointed out Ron. "If madam looks out of her window and spots us hanging about here, she's liable to fling her front door open and start making acerbic remarks. Besides, you'll no doubt be wanting some lunch, so hadn't we better go, so that I can start peeling spuds while you exercise the little grey cells?"

"You definitely have your uses," smiled Tania, giving her husband a light kiss as the couple started off in the direction of home. "But you'd better not be too heavy-handed with the spuds. Don't forget we are expected at Rudolph Wheatley's for tea."

"Good job we're walking, then," responded Ron.

*

"Well, isn't this nice?" observed Rudolph, as the couple settled themselves on to the slightly squeaky leather chesterfield sofa in the historian's drawing room. The room exuded understated Georgian style. The perfectly-proportioned sash window was flanked by curtains in dove-grey damask, and the high white marble mantelpiece bore a pair of urns exquisitely carved from delicately-veined Bluejohn, flanking a Dresden porcelain clock portraying a shepherdess and her swain. The pale mint-green walls were dotted with coloured engravings of hunting scenes and country-house vistas, above wood panelling painted cream. A Turkish carpet occupied the centre of the floor.

"I have to admit, this is something of a treat," continued the historian as he took a seat in a Queen Anne chair upholstered in rose-pink silk. "I so seldom have the chance to entertain."

"I do hope we haven't put you to any trouble," said Tania. "After all, I did practically invite myself."

"Oh, think nothing of it," pooh-poohed Rudolph. "It's just a few cucumber sandwiches. And I hope you like China tea. I have to confess a passion for the old Oolong, a little like Bertie Wooster. Although," he added, casting a look in Ron's direction, "if you prefer, I'm sure I could manage a mug of builder's."

"China tea's fine," Ron reassured him, stifling a smile.

"And ... shall I admit it?" twinkled Rudolph. "I haven't actually made the cake myself. I'm afraid I prevailed upon Sharon from the Holy Grail to create one of her Victoria sponges for me. I hope you won't be disappointed."

"Sharon's cakes never disappoint," declared

Tania.

"I'm so glad," responded Rudolph, leaping to his feet and wheeling forward a tea trolley bearing the refreshments, together with some impossibly dainty Belleek plates, teacups and saucers. "Now, Tania, I don't suppose you'd like to be mother, would you?"

Justice having been done to the sandwiches and cake, the historian leaned forward expectantly. "Now, Tania, I have to say I'm flattered that you want me to come and give another talk at your library. I do so hope that I won't end up boring your patrons."

"I don't see how you could," said Tania. "After all, you'd be talking about a very interesting subject, and I'm sure you must have been very excited when the abbey's new manuscript came to light."

"I was," stated Rudolph. "Can you imagine? There was some sort of initial news story on television, which I will confess I missed – I'm not much of a slave to the box, you know, for all that the people from the TV do quite frequently solicit my opinion on certain matters. But anyway, I hurried to the abbey, and when Cassandra ... oh, do forgive the informality. I mean, of course, the Reverend Milton. Anyway, when the rector showed me the Book of Hours, it took my breath away."

"And you think that you might bore your listeners?" smiled Tania. "I can just see them being caught up in your enthusiasm."

"But then, of course, you encountered something of a problem," said Ron.

Rudolph's face immediately lost its lively expression, which was replaced by a pinched resentfulness. "I assume you are referring to that man Langley."

"Not a fan, then?" enquired Tania delicately.

"Hardly," returned Rudolph. "What on earth possessed the bishop to send the man in to deliver his so-called expert pronouncements on the abbey's new treasure baffles me completely. I can only assume that the bishop had fallen victim to Langley's own estimation of himself, rather than seeking the opinions of those who perhaps knew him better."

"So you knew the professor beforehand, then?" asked Tania, wide-eyed.

"For years, dear lady," said Rudolph. "In fact, far longer than I care to think about."

"And not perhaps the greatest friends?"

"Is it so obvious?" replied Rudolph bitterly. "Not that I blame him for being appointed to an academic chair that should by rights have been mine. Oh no. That would be down to the short-sighted authorities at Camford. But it was the unpleasant way in which he derided any scholarship or research that didn't echo his own narrow views that I found hard to swallow. He was not a nice man. And not only that, but his personal morals left a great deal to be desired. I feel sorry for the rector, having to bear the burden of their personal history." He suddenly seemed to realise that he was possibly divulging information of too confidential a nature. "But please, forget I said that."

"But," said Tania, "I'm a little puzzled. Because I understood, and of course I wouldn't dream of naming any names, but I believe that the professor may have made inappropriate remarks to one of the young men in the abbey community."

"Inappropriate remarks? Is that what we're calling it these days?" retorted Rudolph. "And I should not be surprised in the slightest. He certainly had that reputation when I first knew him. Male, female. Anything with a pulse, not to put too fine a point on it. Never me, of course." A sniff.

"And, your personal feelings aside," said Ron, seeking to bring the conversation back to the matter of the man's death, "from what we hear, it sounds as if Professor Langley was on course to cause problems for the abbey?"

"That is putting it mildly," said Rudolph. "If he had had his way, not only would the new manuscript have been practically stolen from under our noses, but the entire museum would have been closed down. Nothing less than a slap in the face for the whole of Ramston."

"It sounds as if you are not grieving too deeply at his death," suggested Tania.

"I would be lying if I said I were," confirmed the historian.

"And do you have any thoughts as to how it might have come about? Because I'm sure you must know by now that the police are treating it as murder."

"So I believe. And I'm sure that they probably have a plethora of suspects."

"You included?"

Rudolph shrugged nonchalantly. "Why not? I'm doubtless in excellent company."

"So when did you last see the professor?" asked Tania.

"Probably not long before his sad demise," replied Rudolph, a touch of acid in his tone. "We had words, I freely admit. And I was in the abbey at the time, as no doubt the police will discover. Not that I was alone, of course. So were many others. But was I the one who was responsible for his great fall? Well, I think all the king's horses and all the king's men would have a great deal of difficulty proving that."

*

"I honestly don't know what to make of him," confessed Ron, shaking his head, as the couple made their way towards the centre of Ramston. "He certainly makes no secret of his antipathy towards Tarquin

Langley. In fact, he's almost proud of it. And he freely admits that, if the professor had had his way and persuaded the bishop to close down the abbey's museum, he would have powerful motivation to want to do something about it. After all, that museum is very much his baby. So was he taunting us? Was all that 'Yes, I could easily have done it' stuff an elaborate bluff to cover the fact that he was in fact responsible for killing the professor, and he's really not one bit sorry?"

"If he were the only one to consider, then you could be right," replied Tania. "But he isn't. Although he's certainly got the longest history with Langley, so his feelings have had plenty of time to brew and fester. Does that make him a killer?" A shrug. "Too soon to say." She looked around her and took in the route the pair seemed to be taking. "Why are we coming this way? I thought we were heading home."

"And I thought," said Ron, "after all this pate-cudgelling, we ought to have a nice leisurely walk along the river. It's a gorgeous evening. Let's go and look at the ducks, and forget about murder for a bit."

"You have the best ideas," said Tania, linking her arm with her husband's. "It's a shame we didn't snaffle some of that cake. The ducks would have loved it."

Chapter 16
Sunday

Ron was not the only one to whom a pleasant riverside walk had seemed an agreeable way to spend a delightful Sunday evening. The path alongside the river bank was dotted with strolling couples and families, with now and then a black-and-yellow-clad cyclist swerving a precarious way through the pedestrians. On the opposite bank, the rear gardens of picturesque timber-framed cottages fell gradually to the water's edge, their flowerbeds full of colourful traditional English flowers, while there arose from the trees above a perpetual twittering of birds busily commuting back and forth with beakfuls of food for their insistent broods of chicks. In the park along the way, children ran about in pursuit of footballs, their cries piercing the air while their parents, with one eye distractedly upon them, attempted to hold conversations with friends seated on cast-iron benches placed on the tow-path. Dogs zigzagged across the area, cheerfully oblivious to any efforts by their owners to bring them under control. Quacking ducks clustered around a woman and child throwing corn and peas on to the grass. Around the bandstand, a scattering of mostly elderly people seemed to be dozing in the deck chairs remaining after the evening's concert by the town's Boys' Brigade Band, now busily packing up their instruments, while in the war memorial garden a solitary figure, medals proudly gleaming on the breast of his blazer, stood silently contemplating the faded petals of a slowly-disintegrating poppy wreath.

"Buster! Come here, you daft hound, and stop bothering that man! We're over here."

Ron looked down towards his feet, to see a shaggy dog of indeterminate breed seated, ball in mouth, with a hopeful look in its eyes. The dog dropped the ball, nudged it towards Ron's feet with its nose, and look back up with an unmistakeable appeal to throw it.

Tania looked round in the direction of the speaker, to see a pair of young men hastening in her direction. "I thought I recognised that voice," she smiled. "Hello, Robin."

"Oh, hello Tania," replied Robin Barton. "I didn't realise it was you for a minute. Sorry if our dopey dog's been bothering you, but he always wants everyone to join in the game, even if they're total strangers."

"I think it's something about dogs," said Tania. "Don't they say, if you want to make friends, take a dog out for a walk, and that'll do the trick?"

"And I don't mind making friends with this one," said Ron, scruffling the head of his new canine admirer. Prompted by a further nudge to the ball, he picked it up and threw it across the grass. He regarded the animal quizzically as it scampered away. "What is he exactly?"

"He's a pedigree Bitser," laughed Robin. "You know – 'bits o' this, bits o' that'."

"He's a rescue dog," put in Robin's companion. "We got him as a sort of wedding present to ourselves."

"I'm sorry. I should have introduced you," said Tania. "This is my husband Ron. And Ron, I don't know if you've met Robin Barton. He teaches at the Abbey School, and he's forever in my library for something or other. And this is his husband Tom Headley."

The men all shook hands amid friendly nods. "Are you a teacher too, Tom?" enquired Ron.

Tom smiled. "Yes and no. I'm not at the school like Rob. I'm an instructor at Gym Fizz at the industrial estate on the bypass. And I've been working today, so I thought when I got home it would be a good chance to take the dog out for a walk and meet Rob when he finished at the abbey."

"They make you take Sunday classes at school,

Robin?" queried Ron, puzzled. "Isn't that overdoing it a bit?"

"Not the Abbey School," replied Rob. "The abbey itself."

"Rob is part of the bell-ringing team," explained Tania. "Don't you remember, we commented on how lovely the bells sounded on our way here. I suppose that must have been for evensong."

"That's right," nodded Rob. "But, duty done, I'm free as air to enjoy my time doing what I like best." He exchanged fond glances with his husband.

"But it must be quite a commitment for you," said Tania. "I mean, there are all the usual services every day, plus weddings and funerals."

"We have a rota," said Rob. "I'm not on duty all the time. And our rehearsals are usually over by eight."

"Oh, I forgot about rehearsals," remarked Tania casually. "In fact, didn't somebody mention to me that there was a bell-ringing rehearsal the other evening when that awful thing happened with Professor Langley?"

The relaxed expression drained from Rob's face, to be replaced by a look of grim tension. "Actually, yes, there was," he said shortly.

"Did you see him at all?" asked Tania. "I mean, there's no reason why you should, of course, because he would have been in the museum, and I expect you were tied up with your bell-ringing ..."

"As it happens, we did speak," admitted Rob. "Not for long. I had to get away."

"Ah, that's it!" Tania gave a light laugh. "I remember, Adrian Hinton happened to mention that he saw the professor chatting to a young man. That must have been you."

"Chatting!" burst out Tom, who had been standing by but growing visibly more agitated. "I think that's putting a very optimistic spin on it. That bloody professor ... go on, Rob. Tell them."

"I don't really think they want to hear ..." protested Rob.

"That bloody professor made a move on Rob," declared Tom hotly. "In fact, he tried to pressure him into ... well, maybe we ought not to go into details. Foul old creep! And now the word's all round town that not only is he dead, but that somebody shoved him off that museum balcony and killed him. And I'll tell you one thing – if I'd been there at the time, I'd have had great pleasure in doing the deed myself."

"Tom, you shouldn't talk like that," said an uneasy Rob. "Whatever the man tried to do, he's dead now, and that's an end of it. No harm done."

"So when you last saw the professor, he was still alive," Ron sought to clarify.

"Of course he was," replied Rob. "Like I said, I'd only gone back because I'd left something behind in the bell-ringing chamber, so I wanted to get away quickly. And then I went home."

"You went home," echoed Tania.

"Yes."

"After you'd all adjourned to the pub, I expect," said Tom, attempting to lighten the conversation. "That's what you usually do, isn't it? Because I remember, you came in just after I got home at about quarter to ten. I'd only just put my bike away. The pleasures of having to tidy up after late gym classes, eh?" he smiled.

"No, actually I wasn't in the mood for the pub," said Rob awkwardly. "In fact, I'll admit it, I was pretty upset, so I came down here and just sat by the river for a bit. It was quiet, and I wanted to clear my head."

"It is nice and soothing here," agreed Tania. "On a quiet evening, that is." She looked around. "But I suppose we ought to be getting along, and it looks as if your dog has made some new friends." She pointed to where Buster could be seen romping with a gaggle of children dangerously close to the water's edge. "And someone is going to end up falling in if they're not careful."

"Come on, Rob," said Tom. "We'd better go and tether the beast, or else we'll be in trouble. It was nice to see you," he said in farewell, as he drew Rob away in pursuit of their roistering pet.

*

"That was instructive," observed Ron with irony, as he and Tania headed back towards the centre of Ramston.

"How do you mean?"

"Well, for a start, I don't mean that we've got another suspect to add to our list, because I don't think that Tom was making a confession. There is no way that he could have been involved in Langley's death if he was at work at the gym at the time, so the case hasn't got any more complicated than it already was."

"Ah, but hasn't it?" demurred Tania. "Because we've got a time discrepancy. Don't you remember, Robin said that their bell-ringing rehearsal ended at eight or thereabouts, but Tom told us that Rob didn't get home until after nine forty-five. That's a big gap."

"But Rob accounted for that," pointed out Ron. "He said he came down and sat in the park to unwind from the stress of that encounter with Tarquin Langley. And I don't really blame him – I'd probably have done much the same thing in his shoes."

"But what if he didn't unwind?" countered Tania. "What if he stayed wound up, to the extent that he went back to the abbey to tell the professor what he thought of him? And that meeting ended in violence?"

Ron considered. "It's plausible. Two problems. One, nobody's mentioned seeing Robin back in the abbey after the initial ... let's call it 'conversation' ... between him and Langley, as witnessed by both Louise and Adrian. Two, how did he get back in? We know the racket the Jerusalem Porch door makes. And isn't that the only entrance for visitors? Surely it would have drawn somebody's attention if it had sounded off again?"

Tania pulled a face. "I don't want it to be Robin. But you must admit that the police would definitely consider that his motive was worth looking into, once they find out the facts. And I can't think that they won't emerge."

"Means and motive I grant you," said Ron, "but the opportunity aspect is still looking a bit dodgy. Anyway, we were supposed to be giving thoughts of the murder a bit of a rest. I brought you down here to commune with the ducks, not to interview a suspect."

Tania laughed. "Okay, you win. So how about popping in to the Cross Keys for a nice relaxing drink?" Ron gave her a look. "And I promise not to start cross-examining Dennis Dean to see if he can shed any more light on what he's already told us. Cross my heart!"

"I believe you," said Ron. "Mind you, having viewed your consummate acting performance at Rudolph Wheatley's house, I'm not sure that I should. All that innocent fluttering of the eyelashes!"

"I shall go nowhere near the bar," promised Tania.

"Rats!" retorted Ron. "I suppose that means I'm paying."

*

The couple emerged into the twilit Market Square and stood for a few moments gazing up at the bulk of the abbey rising before them. As they watched, they could see the majority of the internal lights down the length of the nave being turned off one by one, leaving only a faint gleam from a single light source at the east end. Seconds later, the exit door in the south transept opened, and a figure exited, trotting across the square and evidently heading for the convenience store alongside the Cross Keys.

Tania nudged Ron. “Look,” she hissed. “It's Peter Hawkley. This is too good an opportunity to miss.”

“Oh no,” groaned Ron. “Haven't you done enough detecting for one day?”

“Shush,” murmured Tania. “Strike while the suspect is hot. Hello, Peter!” she cried, as the figure was about to pass the pair. “You seem in a hurry.”

Peter juddered to a halt. “Sorry?” He peered at the couple. “Oh, it's you, Tania. I didn't notice you for a second. My mind was a million miles away.”

“Obviously focussed on your mission,” smiled Ron. “Because you do look as if you are intent on something of great importance.”

Peter chuckled. “Hardly. And it's my own stupid fault. I was going around putting the lights out in the abbey before locking up, and the batteries in my torch suddenly died. I knew they were running out, but I forgot to replace them earlier, so I was just nipping into Mary's Market to pick up a fresh pack. Otherwise I'd be stumbling about in the dark and crashing into things over there.”

“No, you could easily hurt yourself,” said Tania solicitously. “And we don't want any more accidents, not after what happened to that poor Professor Langley, do we?” She gave a brief sideways glance towards her husband.

“But it doesn't seem as if it was an accident, does it?” Ron picked up his cue instantly. “Don't you remember, love, we've heard that the police have some information which proves that it seems to be murder.”

“Of course! You're right,” replied Tania. “I can't get my head around the fact that a murder could happen in our own abbey. Mind you ...” she lowered her voice. “I wouldn't usually listen to rumours, but isn't it true that the professor was making himself no friends at all, for all that he'd only been in town five minutes?"

"Um ... yes ... actually, the rumours are true, Tania," admitted Peter reluctantly. He seemed unwilling to go into any further details.

"Oh, now, you can't just say that and leave it hanging. There must be more," coaxed Tania. "And it's obviously all to do with the Book of Hours that's just been found. Wasn't the professor sent in by the bishop to examine it?"

"He was," said Peter. "And what he was saying about the book, and the abbey in general, was all very unflattering. I mean, I only heard a few snippets, but he disparaged Mr Wheatley's exhibition in no uncertain terms, and I think there was even a threat to remove it all together and take everything lock, stock and barrel to the cathedral at Westchester. And not only that, although that was bad enough," continued Peter, warming to his theme, "he even had the temerity to criticise Sharon's catering in the Holy Grail café, and he went on to take great delight in lambasting Heather's choice of stock for her souvenir shop. Heather, of all people! I ask you. She's one of the nicest people I know. She didn't deserve that. I heard it all, but they didn't notice me. People don't because I'm always around."

"It does sound as if Professor Langley was on a deliberate mission to damage the abbey's reputation," remarked Ron. "I can see why that would upset you."

"Yes, it did," agreed Peter sombrely.

"And, of course, you would have been on the premises when the professor fell," observed Tania. "Do you know what actually happened?"

"Nobody seems to," replied Peter. "It was just before we closed for the evening, so I was on my way all round the abbey checking that there weren't any leftover visitors in any of the out-of-the-way corners. And there's always somebody from the abbey community somewhere about. I remember seeing Pandora Weston at one point, and Robin Barton was to and fro as well. I always make a point of finishing off by checking the crypt under the chancel, because it's surprising how often there's someone down there who's lost track of time. And then there was a scream, and I came up from down below to see people converging from all directions. And there was Louise standing over the body beneath the museum parapet."

"But nobody seems to have seen the professor fall, from what I've heard," said Ron. "And there must have been some sort of argument leading up to it. But you heard nothing?"

"No. It must have happened just a couple of minutes beforehand."

"But it could only have been one of the people in the abbey, surely," suggested Ron. "And apart from you, who would that have been?"

"The rector, of course. I believe she must have been in the vestry, because she emerged from that direction behind me. Heather too – she came from the direction of the shop, and I saw the rector almost push her aside. And I think Mr Wheatley came out of one of the side chapels, but I can't be sure. It's all a bit of a blur."

"You saw and heard nobody else?" enquired Tania.

Peter shook his head. "No. And surely nobody could believe that one of them could have been responsible." As the abbey clock chimed the half hour, he gave a start. "Goodness, the time. I have to hurry, or I'll be late with my duties. Must go." Without another word, he darted into the convenience store, as Tania and Ron resumed their leisurely progress across the square in the direction of the Cross Keys. As they were about to enter,

Tania looked over her shoulder, to see Peter trotting back towards the abbey and disappearing inside through the small door in the transept.

"Ron!" Tania clutched her husband's arm.

"What?"

"I've just realised, we've got it all wrong."

"We have? How?"

"Well, not all wrong," said Tania. "But we were ruling out Pandora and Robin because, as far as we knew, they had left the abbey before the professor died."

"That's right."

"And we said they couldn't have got back in without being detected, on account of the noise the door of the Jerusalem Porch makes when it closes."

"Yes, I remember saying so. That door weighs a ton, and no matter how hard I've tried to close it quietly in the past, it always makes an almighty 'clonk' just at the end."

"But they could have got back in," insisted Tania. "We've just seen Peter go back inside through the little exit door by Heather's shop. And it's not even as if there's a turnstile there to stop unauthorised access. It's just that the vast majority of people don't realise they can get in that way because they're always directed towards the official entrance in the Jerusalem Porch."

"And Robin, knowing the abbey well, would probably be aware of that." Ron took up the thought. "And who's to say that Pandora didn't know about it as well? She could have noticed the fact when she left the abbey earlier. So those two are back in the mix."

Chapter 17
Monday

"What's all this then?" enquired a surprised Ron, as he entered the bedroom with the early morning tray of tea to find his wife browsing through the wardrobe and picking out her clothes for the day. "You aren't due at work for hours yet."

"I know that," replied Tania, "but I had an idea. I don't want to leave talking to the other people who might have some involvement with Tarquin Langley's death longer than I have to, so I thought I'd make an early start this morning before I go to the library."

"So what's the plan?"

"I believe they have an early service at the abbey at half past eight in the morning, which I assume the rector will be conducting. I'm guessing that it ought to be over not long after nine o'clock, so that should give me the chance to have a word with her before I have to go on to work."

"If she'll speak to you. I shouldn't be at all surprised if the police haven't heavily suggested that none of the abbey staff speak to any unauthorised personnel about the professor. And when I say the police, I mean Inspector Copper, and if you don't come under the heading of 'unauthorised personnel' I shall be very surprised. You saw the look in the inspector's eye."

"Yes, darling," said Tania, adopting her most innocent expression. "But I'm not going to be investigating, am I? I'm just intending to have a chat with a friend who must surely be upset at the turn things have taken."

"Devious woman," muttered Ron. "But in the meantime, come back to bed and drink your tea. We've got plenty of time before we need to leave."

"We?"

"You don't think I'm going to let you go on your own, do you?" asked Ron with determination. "And miss the fun of watching the great detective at work? Not likely."

*

The worshippers were filing out of the Jerusalem Porch as Tania and Ron sidled past them on their way into the abbey, coming face to face with Louise Froyle amidst the throng.

"Oh Tania dear, you're a bit late for the service," chuckled the old woman. "Forget to set your alarm, did you?"

"Oh, we haven't come for the service," answered Tania.

"Well, I must say, that doesn't come as a complete surprise, dear, seeing as I've never seen you in the congregation at this time of day. Or at all, to be honest, not meaning to be unkind."

"I'm afraid you've caught us out there, Louise," smiled Ron. "You'll know all the regulars, of course. And I suspect you attend more services than the rest of us put together."

"I like to be ready," replied Louise. "None of us knows the time when we shall be called, do we?"

"True," said Tania.

"Anyway, what brings you here at this hour?" asked Louise. "We aren't open for visitors yet, you know."

"Oh, Tania just wanted a quick word with the rector about ... something," said Ron evasively. "Do you happen to know where she is?"

"She's just inside. She always makes a point of saying goodbye to everyone at the door after the service. You should just catch her. And I must get on myself. I need to go and have my usual Monday chat with the florist to see what he's got in this week." The elderly lady bustled out towards the exit.

"Oh, hello Tania," said Cassandra Milton with some surprise, as the couple approached her just as she was shaking hands with the last of the departing parishioners. "And Ron." She looked uncertain. "Am I expecting you? Or have I forgotten an appointment? Because, to be honest," she confessed with a wan smile, "what with everything that's happened of late, I'm afraid I'm not quite as organised as I would normally be."

"Oh no, nothing of the kind," Tania reassured her. "It's just that ... well, working in the library as I do, I'm always being asked about everything under the sun, and of course you can guess what today's chief topic of conversation will be. So I thought you might be able to tell me what I can sensibly say to people when they ask. Especially as, you know, the professor's death is now being treated as murder by the police. And we all want to keep the damage to the abbey's reputation as limited as possible, don't we?"

"I see," said Cassandra. She looked around. "Perhaps we'd better not talk here. And I need to change." She indicated her surplice. "Why don't you come through to the vestry, and we can talk then." She turned and led the way down the nave towards the vestry, Tania and Ron in her wake.

The rector waved absent-mindedly towards a pair of chairs in front of her desk, before turning away and divesting herself of her white outer garment, which she stowed away in one of the massive oaken cupboards lining one wall of the lofty stone-vaulted room. As she subsided into the substantial carved wooden chair behind the desk, she looked weary, and she unconsciously fingered the silver pectoral cross on its chain around her neck as she gazed at her visitors. She raised eyebrows above dark-circled eyes. "Well, Tania?"

Tania cleared her throat uncertainly. "I suppose I really ought to apologise, rector," she began.

Cassandra seemed taken aback by the remark. "I can't see what you would have to apologise for, Tania."

"I feel as if I've brought trouble upon you," said Tania with a sigh. "If I hadn't been so determined to go ferreting into matters which really aren't any of my business, the facts about what happened to Professor Langley might never have come to light."

The rector gave another wan smile. "You can't expect me to agree. Whatever happens, the truth must be known. No matter who is hurt in the process."

"And coming on the heels of all the good news about finding the Book of Hours," put in Ron. "It's such a shame that the shine has been taken off it by the professor's death. Sorry ... but I suppose we have to call it 'murder'."

"Yes," agreed the rector heavily.

"There must be people wondering if it was more than an unhappy coincidence that it was Professor Langley that the bishop called in," said Tania. "Because of course, as I think you mentioned, you knew him before, didn't you?"

"I did," said Cassandra. She did not seem disposed to say any more, but as Tania continued simply to gaze at her, she reluctantly added, "He was a tutor when I was studying at Camford."

"Then I can see why you would be upset at the death of such a close friend," nodded Tania with sympathy.

"Not close," insisted the rector with surprisingly strong emphasis. "We hadn't seen one another in years."

"Oh. I'm sorry. My mistake. Because I was under the impression that ..." Tania let the thought hang. "I suppose a close friend wouldn't have presented a threat to the abbey's peace and quiet in the way that Professor Langley seems to have done."

"Why? What have you heard?" Cassandra's voice

betrayed tension.

"I think," said Ron, "that the professor wasn't making himself popular with those who work around the abbey. Wasn't there even talk that the Book of Hours, and even the whole museum itself, were under threat of being taken away completely? At the very least, that must have ruffled some feathers."

Tania turned to her husband. "Yes, Ron, but ruffled feathers do not necessarily lead to murder. There must have been more to it than that." She faced the rector once again. "Of course, I don't suppose you would have any suspicions yourself as to who might have been responsible?"

Cassandra shook her head. "No," she stated firmly.

"But it would have to have been someone who was in and around the abbey shortly before the body was discovered," mused Tania. "Tell me, when would you have last seen the professor?"

The rector appeared to cast her mind back. "Perhaps about an hour before Louise found him. I'd gone up to the museum because I wanted to know his latest thoughts on our new discovery, but he was reluctant to be definite, so I simply came back down here. I had some paperwork to attend to."

"And the next thing you knew, presumably, was Louise's scream?" said Ron.

"It was. I made my way to the scene as quickly as I could – I remember pushing past Heather, and Peter was also somewhere behind me - and it was decided that the police must be called. And that really is all I can tell you about the matter."

"Until, that is, I drew the detective inspector's attention to what I'd noticed up in the museum," said Tania. "Has he spoken to you again since?"

"Not since Saturday," replied Cassandra. "In fact,

he said that he would be back to interview all concerned this morning. I'm expecting a phone call at some time. But he did ask me not to discuss the case with anyone in the meantime."

"Oh dear," said Tania with an embarrassed laugh. "I suppose that means me. I do hope I won't have got you into hot water with him. Perhaps you'd better not mention our little chat to him."

"The seal of the confessional?" enquired the rector with a faint wry smile.

"Something like that," said Ron, getting to his feet. "And we'd better be making a move, love. It must be almost time for you to open the library, and the rector must have plenty to do, so we'll be on our way." He turned as if to head for the door back out into the nave.

"You'll be quicker going out this way," said Cassandra, standing and producing a small key from her pocket. She turned around and drew aside a curtain, to reveal a small concealed door. "It's my own private entrance," she explained. "It leads straight out into the Market Square. It will save you going the long way round via the Jerusalem Porch." She unlocked the door and held it open for the couple, who found themselves standing in the shadow of one of the abbey's main buttresses, directly opposite the Ramston library.

"I'm not sure whether that told us anything fresh," said Tania.

"And even if it did, we haven't got time to dissect it now," stated Ron, as the abbey clock could be heard beginning to chime. "Look at the time. Duty calls, at least for you."

"You're right," said Tania. "But I really did want to try and have a word with Heather Clanville, especially as the police are likely to be stomping around the abbey today. I would particularly like to avoid Inspector Copper's disapproving gaze if I possibly can."

"Then here's a thought. Why don't I come back at lunchtime so that we can pop over to the Holy Grail for something to eat? Surely the inspector couldn't object to that. And if we happen to run into Heather during the course of our visit ..." Ron grinned.

"And you have the gall to call me devious," laughed Tania. "Right. See you then." A quick peck on the cheek and she hurried in the direction of the library front door.

*

"This is becoming a habit with you two," smiled Sharon Burley as Tania and Ron entered the Holy Grail café at lunchtime. "Would you like me to put a notice on your favourite corner table saying 'Permanently Reserved'?"

"It's our own silly fault," replied Tania, affecting a slight blush. "We were rushing about first thing, because we had to ... do one thing and another ... so I completely forgot to make myself something to bring to work for lunch, and then Ron got caught up with work and completely lost track of time until he suddenly started to feel hungry, so we decided to treat ourselves and pop in here for a couple of your lovely paninis."

"You could do a lot worse," said Sharon complacently. "And you know it's always a pleasure to see you, specially on a Monday, because we're usually quiet. So, what is it you fancy?"

The orders placed, the couple were about to make their way to their table when Tania turned back. "I ... er ... I don't suppose you've seen Heather from the shop today, have you?" she enquired with elaborate nonchalance.

"Oh, what a shame," said Sharon. "You've just missed her. She was in only a few minutes ago. She took something because she said she was going to have a working snack. Did you want her for anything special?"

"Oh no," said Ron. "Just wondered how she was, what with, you know, everything that's gone on."

"She seemed surprisingly perky," said Sharon. "Happiest I've seen her for a while. Just goes to show, you never can tell, can you?"

"Absolutely not," replied Tania. "Anyway, I'm looking forward to that panini, so we'd better not keep you talking."

Their lunch consumed at almost indecent speed, and with a hasty farewell to Sharon, the pair left the café and made their way down towards the abbey's souvenir shop, where they found Heather Clanville, feather duster in hand, busily dusting the glass shelving holding some of her sales items. A part-eaten sandwich lay on a plate next to the till.

"Good afternoon, Heather," called Tania as the couple entered the shop.

Heather whirled round and greeted the newcomers with a bright smile. "Tania! Ron! How lovely to see you. I was just in the middle of sprucing up my shop display, ready for the new week's visitors. How are you?"

"We're very well," responded Tania, somewhat surprised at the cheery welcome. "More to the point, how are you?"

"Never better," smiled Heather. "You won't mind if I get on with this, will you? Did you come in for anything in particular?"

"No, not really," said Ron. "We just wondered ... er ..."

Tania thought swiftly. "We just wondered if you knew when there might be a new edition of the guide to the abbey. Because I'm sure Rudolph Wheatley must already be thinking about revising the existing guide, what with the discovery of the Book of Hours and everything."

"I expect so," said Heather. "But I'm afraid I don't know anything. I haven't actually seen Mr Wheatley since ..." She stopped short, and her smile faded.

"You mean since Professor Langley died?" said Tania. "No, I suppose things haven't really been normal since then. Especially as the police are now certain that it was murder."

"They were here earlier on," said Heather, her voice slightly shaky. "You know, that inspector, asking questions."

"And were you able to tell him anything helpful?" asked Ron.

Heather switched a determined smile back on. "No, not a thing. I told him I saw nothing at the time, so I think he was rather disappointed."

"At the time, you say," said Tania. "But of course, you would have told him about the things the professor had to say to you beforehand. About the shop, I mean. Especially shortly before he died."

"How do you ...?" Heather stopped short. "But I was nowhere near at the time. And anyway, I didn't really think it was worth bothering the inspector with details of the few remarks the professor may have made," she continued. "And besides, it's all irrelevant now, isn't it? The professor's gone. So I'm just carrying on with my job looking after the visitors' needs when they want a little something to remember their visit to the abbey. And every sale I make helps to keep the abbey going, and that makes me very happy." The bright smile was back. "And now, I suppose, I'd better get on. These shelves won't dust themselves, will they? You never know when I'm going to be inundated with customers. And I expect you've probably got lots to do yourselves."

Tania and Ron exchanged glances at the not-so-subtle hint. "You're right, of course," said Ron. "Those spreadsheets of mine won't produce themselves either, will they? We'll be off."

"Bye then. Oh, and Tania, I'll be sure to let you know as soon as I have anything about a new abbey guide book," said Heather. She turned back to her work, humming softly, as her visitors made their way out of the exit door and back on to the Market Square.

"Well, that's a bit of a transformation from the last reports we heard about Heather from Sharon and Dennis," mused Ron. "There she was in a state, which if what we've heard about the professor's pronouncements about her shop is completely understandable, and now we find her, seemingly as happy as Larry, with a song on her lips. Something has wrought a considerable change over the lady."

"Maybe it's the fact that the sword of Damocles which Langley was dangling over the abbey, and consequently over her shop, has been very efficiently removed by his death. Maybe it's just that the tension has suddenly gone."

"You could be right," agreed Ron. "But she does seem unnaturally happy. Is it remotely possible that she did deliver that killer blow, and she's gone slightly hysterical over the fact?"

"Madder things have been known," admitted Tania. "But surely nobody would ever think that Heather was the murderous type."

"Is there a murderous type?" queried Ron. "And if there is, where do the others fit into it? The rector? Peter? Rudolph, or your friend Robin. Or our author of murder mysteries herself?"

"It's one of them," replied Tania. "And all we have to do is work out which."

Chapter 18
Monday/Tuesday

"Your brow is very furrowed, love," remarked Ron, as he emerged from the kitchen.

Tania gave a slightly troubled smile in response. "I've spent the whole afternoon thinking about who could have killed the professor. In fact, I've been so distracted that one of our visitors asked me if I could suggest some tasteful fiction suitable for her thirteen-year-old daughter, and I recommended Mary Berry."

"Oh dear," chuckled Ron. "But I suggest you leave all thoughts of murder to one side for the moment and come and have some supper. The timer has just pinged."

"That's it!" cried Tania. "That's what I need to do."

"What? Eat? Sounds logical to me," grinned Ron. "A detective marches on her stomach, or something like that."

"Idiot," riposted Tania fondly. "No. Timing, that's the key. If I can sort out a timeline for who was where and when, then surely that's going to give us a solution."

Ron nodded in agreement. "Good plan. But first," he added firmly, "supper, or the cook will become very cross through feeling under-appreciated."

"Heaven forbid," said Tania. "And I don't suppose a glass of wine will do any harm."

"I like your thinking," said Ron. "And now, if madame will come this way, your table awaits."

By common consent, the subject of the death at the abbey was assiduously avoided during the course of the meal. "But," smiled Ron as he cleared the plates, "for no particular reason, your thought processes on that matter which shall not be named might be lubricated by a further drop or two of Château Whatnot."

"We could do worse," agreed Tania.

Supper over, the couple settled cosily on the sofa,

the remains of the wine in glasses at their sides.

"Now," said Ron, "how do you want to proceed? You said something about sorting out a timeline for the evening of the murder."

"I did," replied Tania. "Because I can't see any reason why we shouldn't use the traditional approach to solving a crime by looking at the means, motive, and opportunity."

"Fine," nodded Ron. "And we've pretty much covered the first two already. Means – we're pretty sure that the stone ceiling boss was what was used to deliver that lethal whack to the head which killed the professor."

"Agreed. Although we can't be absolutely certain without the forensic report on the bloodstain on the boss, which I'm betting Inspector Copper has by now. But let's take it as read."

"Blood-red, in fact" quipped Ron. Tania gave him a look. "So, moving swiftly on. Again, as to motives, we're quite confident that we've got plenty to look at. Professor Langley was fairly comprehensive in his ability to set people against him. The abbey staff, chiefly - the rector ... Heather Clanville ... Peter Hawkley ... Robin Barton. He even managed to have a snipe at Sharon Burley. And that's not to mention the two outsiders, Pandora Weston and Rudolph Wheatley."

"But there are other insiders I'm sure we can confidently rule out," pointed out Tania. "He doesn't seem to have had any sort of run-in with Adrian Hinton or Louise Froyle, so there's surely no motive there. And as for Sharon, nobody's mentioned seeing her out and about round the abbey, apart from her tea delivery to Adrian. And if she was up to her elbows cleaning that oven, then that's not a five-minute job."

"Rubber gloves?" murmured Ron. "No fingerprints on the murder weapon?"

"Nobody kills someone because they get a bad

review for their sticky buns!" declared Tania firmly. "And anyway, she was the first one to flag up to us that there was something amiss. Why would she do that if she had anything to do with the professor's death? No, she's out."

"Leaving us with just our six. So can we follow their movements on that evening?"

"I think we can. Just let me ..." Tania reached for her notebook on the side table. She took a preparatory sip of wine before starting to leaf through the pages. "This is going to be a bit of a fiddle, because I'm going to have to go to and fro, but we'll do our best. And I think we have to start with Dennis Dean."

"How so?"

"Because that's the first time reference we have. Tarquin Langley was busily going about getting up everyone's nose during the day, but we know that Dennis booked him a table in the Cross Keys restaurant for six-thirty."

"And we also know," put in Ron, "that Pandora Weston was in there for an early supper when they opened, so that would be five-thirty."

"Which," continued Tania, "puts her finishing her meal at the same time as the professor arrived for his. So after the two had their little spat ..."

"Not so little," remarked Ron drily.

"... Pandora headed over to the abbey at about twenty to seven, according to Dennis."

"Right. And, also according to Dennis, Cassandra Milton turned up in the restaurant a little later ..."

"Hold on." Tania riffled through the pages of her notebook. "That's just after seven, and after she'd had her own little confrontation with Tarquin Langley, she left, presumably to head back over to the abbey herself. So let's call that around ten past seven."

"That sounds fair. What a good job Dennis keeps a close eye on what's going on in his pub," observed Ron.

"Because we can also be pretty certain that it was around twenty to eight that the professor left the restaurant. Presumably to join the merry throng congregating in the abbey," he added with a grim smile.

"We know he did," said Tania, leafing through her notebook once again. "Because Adrian Hinton told us that he overheard Pandora Weston and Tarquin Langley going at it again, and we've got that noted for just after seven-forty, so that all ties in. And it's after that argument that we have Pandora stating that she left the abbey."

"Allegedly," pointed out Ron. "There's no supporting evidence either way."

"Allegedly," agreed Tania. "And absence of evidence is not evidence of absence."

"So then we're coming on towards eight o'clock."

"Which is when the rector says she was in the vestry talking to that engaged couple about their wedding arrangements."

"And Louise Froyle confirmed that when we spoke to her, so we can be pretty certain that that's correct."

"True," said Tania. "And she also told us that it was shortly after that, so let's say five past eight, after she'd been chatting to Peter Hawkley at his desk, that the professor was involved with some sort of interaction with Robin Barton."

"Interaction? Is that what we're calling it?" queried Ron. "It sounded to me, from what Louise told us she overheard, more like a very unpleasant case of blackmail."

"And wasn't that confirmed by Adrian Hinton?" asked Tania. "Not that he could have heard anything from his perch in the organ loft, but he certainly saw Robin's reaction. But again, Robin told us that he left the abbey almost immediately after that. And he said he went home."

"Ah, but we now know that he didn't, don't we?" stated Ron. "It practically had to be dragged out of him, but he said he went to the park for some quiet thinking, and only went home later. And we've got nobody to verify his movements. Unfortunately for him."

"Mmm." Tania looked pensive. "So let's get back to some movements we can verify. Again, Louise mentioned that she saw the rector heading up towards the museum at around eight-thirty, which is when she heard the professor threatening to wash some of the dirty linen from her past in public. But we don't know where either of them went after that particular confrontation, or when."

"Actually, that's not strictly true," pointed out Ron. "Didn't Adrian tell us something about words passing between the professor and Rudolph Wheatley at some point after that? Haven't you got something in your notes about that?"

"Let me take a look." Tania once again thumbed through the pages of her notebook. "You're right. Well remembered. According to Adrian, he was an unwilling witness to another of Tarquin Langley's tirades, this time against Rudolph when he was ensconced in one of the little chantry chapels. That was at about nine o'clock, the same time as he saw Peter Hawkley up in the tower, so presumably going around the museum. He must have been taking advantage of the professor's absence to do his rounds that he told us about."

"Ending up in the crypt."

"And that brings us on to nine-twenty-five, which Sharon gives us as the time of the professor's death, just before the abbey's closing time."

"Or at least, the time of the discovery of the body," remarked Ron. "The two aren't identical."

Tania shook her head in frustration. "There must

be something that doesn't tally," she said. "I remember reading something in a book once ..."

"There's a surprise," grinned Ron.

"No. And just for a change, it wasn't a detective novel. Although it was, in a way."

"Has this all been too much for you, love?" enquired Ron solicitously. "Because you're starting to talk gibberish."

Tania sighed. "Sorry," she smiled. "No, this was an autobiography by a former policeman. A detective with the Met. He was talking about his career, and some of the cases he'd been involved with ..."

"Names changed to protect the guilty, I imagine," put in Ron.

"Something like that. Anyway, he said that no two cases were ever the same, and you always had to have a fresh approach each time. But there was one factor that was usually present in anything like a murder case where you had several suspects, and they were all giving their accounts of what their involvement was."

"And this magical ingredient was ...?"

"Inconsistency. There was very often one fact, which might be the most trivial thing, but if you could spot it, it could be the key. Something that could not be true. And I swear it's there, somewhere."

Ron put his arm around his wife's shoulder. "It'll come to you, love," he murmured comfortingly. He glanced at his watch. "But for now, I suggest you give your brain a rest. Have you noticed the time? So I recommend a good long soak in a hot bath, and then I will bring you up a cup of my finest cocoa. My spies tell me that Miss Marple used to swear by a nice relaxing cup of cocoa at bedtime. And then you can sleep on it, and who knows?"

Tania snuggled into her husband's embrace.

"You're good to me."

"I have my uses," replied Ron lightly. He got to his feet. "I'll start that bath running."

*

Ron closed the book on his lap, preparatory to putting it aside and switching out the bedside lamp. He took a last fond look at his wife alongside him as she lay there, apparently asleep, snuffling faintly, her eyes moving rapidly beneath closed lids.

Suddenly, Tania's eyes shot open, and she sat up abruptly. "I've got it!"

"Good grief, woman!" exclaimed Ron. "You almost gave me a heart attack. I thought you were asleep."

Tania blinked. "I was ... I think. I must have been. Anyway, it's all your fault."

"What is?"

"Tarquin Langley's murder. Well, the solution, anyway. You suggested I sleep on it. Well, I have done."

"And the solution to the crime came to you miraculously in a dream?"

"Don't be facetious. I don't know how it happened. But don't they say that the unconscious mind can work wonders?"

Ron gave a faint groan. "And I was just about to be blissfully unconscious myself," he murmured. "Anyway, is this really the time for a discussion about the workings of the human mind? Just tell me who did it."

"Well ..." hesitated Tania.

"Oh, come on," urged Ron. "If you think you know, say so."

"But when it's a friend ..." She seemed in an agony of indecision, before declaring firmly, "No. I want to go through everything first, one more time, to make sure that I'm not accusing someone unfairly. Because if I did, you'd never look at them the same way ever again. And if we were to say anything and I turned out to be wrong, I'd never forgive myself. I must speak to Inspector Copper before I do anything."

Ron raised an eyebrow. "Well, you're not going to do that tonight, are you, love?" he enquired reasonably. "I'm not at all sure he'd take too kindly to getting a call from someone he obviously thinks of as some mad amateur detective woman at this hour. It's almost midnight. Anyway, you don't have his number."

"I could get it," retorted Tania, but then she relaxed back into her pillow. "But you're right. I'm being stupid. But first thing in the morning, I'm going to look at all our notes again. Just to make sure I'm right."

"And in the meantime, you leave me twisting in the wind? You do realise that I'm not going to sleep a wink now, don't you?"

"Sorry, darling." Tania propped herself up once more and leaned over to kiss her husband. "If only there were some way we could relax you to take your mind off it."

"I have a funny feeling you're not talking about cocoa," smiled Ron, as he slid down into the bed.

*

"There you are, love. Second cup." Ron placed the mug of tea in front of his wife and then settled himself across the breakfast table from her. He gazed at her over the paperwork spread across the tabletop between them. "So, you're absolutely sure about this?" he pressed.

Tania nodded reluctantly. "I'm afraid so. Horrible as it seems."

"So now what?"

"I'm going to call the inspector. He must be at his desk by now. It's gone nine."

"I'm not sure they keep regular office hours in the police, love," smiled Ron. "But go ahead. If you can find his number."

"For goodness' sake, I'm a librarian!" retorted Tania. "We know how to look things up. Pass me my phone." Ron handed the mobile across the table. "I'm sure the inspector must be based at the County Police Headquarters in Westchester, so therefore ..." A sequence of dabs at the phone screen. "And there's their number. So ..." She pressed the 'dial' icon. "Oh, hello. I wonder if you could put me through to Detective Inspector Copper please. I assume he is based there? ... Oh good. May I speak to him, please? ... It's about a case he's investigating ... The one at Ramston Abbey. The murder ... But I have some information for him ... Of course. My name's Tania Faye ... Yes, I'll hold." There followed a series of clicks.

"*Mrs Faye,*" came the inspector's voice in wary tones. "*This is unexpected. What can I do for you?*"

Tania cleared her throat, suddenly filled with uncertainty. "Actually, inspector, it's more of a matter of what I can do for you."

"*According to the switchboard, you say you have some information for me.*"

"Well ... it's more like a solution, really. You see, I've been thinking the whole business of Professor Langley's death through, and from what people have said to me ..."

"*Mrs Faye!*" The exasperation in Inspector Copper's voice was plain to hear as he cut her off. "*This is a police matter. And I thought I had made myself clear when I told you that I really did not appreciate your interventions in a case I am conducting, however well-intentioned they may be.*"

"Yes, but ..."

"*Furthermore, and I don't know if you're aware of this, Sergeant Radley and I made another visit to Ramston yesterday ...*"

"Yes, I did know that, but ..."

"*... and we conducted extensive further interviews with the individuals most concerned with the case,*" pressed on the detective, *"so I think it's highly unlikely that there is anything fresh which you can bring to the table. The case remains ongoing."*

"Inspector!" Tania was not to be intimidated. "If you will just listen for a moment."

There was a long pause, followed by a deep sigh. *"I'm sorry, Mrs Faye. I know you mean well, but ..."*

"The thing is, inspector, that when I talk to people, they aren't on their guard as they probably are when you're interviewing them. So odd little things slip out. Do you see what I mean?"

"I do," admitted Copper guardedly.

"And I expect that whenever you're investigating a case, you always look for some sort of inconsistency in what people tell you, because that can point towards finding out who may not be telling the truth."

A reluctant chuckle was audible at the other end of the line. *"It sounds as if you've been doing your homework, Mrs Faye."*

"And that's what I wanted to tell you about, inspector. Because if I've been told two things which can't possibly both be true, then that's bound to be important. Agreed?"

"Agreed. So perhaps you can tell me where all this is leading."

Tania took a deep breath. "I know who killed Tarquin Langley."

*

"I still can't believe you coaxed Inspector Copper into doing this." Ron could not keep a note of admiration out of his voice.

"I'm a very persuasive woman." Tania was unable to stifle a smile as she sipped her gin and tonic in the lounge bar of the Cross Keys. "Besides, he freely admitted that there was no way that he could have got people to repeat the conversations they'd had with us verbatim, and he couldn't attempt to put forward hearsay as evidence to his superiors."

"And I reckon what clinched it was your suggestion that he have a word with Inspector Tregarth in Cornwall. Obviously that was what convinced him that your way of telling the story with everybody there was going to be most productive in terms of getting a confession."

"I suspect the chance of wrapping up the case without devoting too many police man-hours to it was also a factor," said Tania. She gave a slight shrug. "Do you suppose I'm doing the right thing?" she asked, her voice suddenly filled with doubt. "What if I've got it wrong?"

"You haven't," Ron reassured her. "You convinced me, and now you've convinced the inspector. And I'm sure he believes that this is the least dramatic way of bringing things to an end."

"I hope so," said Tania. She looked across at the clock above the bar. "Time's getting on. Evensong must be almost over, so the abbey will be emptying out soon."

"Which is why Inspector Copper told everyone that he wanted people to gather in the Holy Grail afterwards, so that he could follow up on some of the details from his visit yesterday," said Ron. "And he's going to interview you as if you were one of the suspects?"

"Because I was the one who discovered the murder weapon," nodded Tania. "And that gives me a chance to explain a few things."

Ron gave a quiet chuckle. "Inspector Copper evidently isn't as fierce as he'd probably like some people to think," he observed. "He's actually quite subtle in his own way."

As if to prove Tania's time calculations right, the door to the bar opened, and a small group of people entered, obviously fresh from the evening service.

Ron downed the remains of his pint and got to his feet. “Come on, love,” he said, holding out his hand to his wife. “I'm guessing that what is about to happen is going to come as a relief to more than one person.”

Chapter 19
Tuesday

Tania blinked in slight surprise at the number of people occupying the Holy Grail, making it seem crowded. Seated at the various tables were several of the abbey's regulars, with Adrian Hinton alongside Robin Barton, who was unexpectedly accompanied by his husband Tom Headley. Louise Froyle occupied an adjacent table, darting sharp beady-eyed looks around the room and ignoring the murmured remarks from Peter Hawkley next to her. Rudolph Wheatley lounged against one wall, casting his languid gaze over the assembly, while Pandora Weston sat solitary, tense and upright, her eyes fixed front. In a corner, half-concealed by a pillar, Heather Clanville seemed to be trying to make herself as unobtrusive as possible, as Sharon Burley, in her customary place behind the counter, appeared to be occupying herself in making a tray of drinks for the company. As Ron and Tania entered, all eyes swivelled towards them, and they took their seats at an unoccupied table in uncomfortable silence.

After a few moments, the door from the church opened once again, and Cassandra Milton ushered Detective Inspector Copper into the room, with Detective Sergeant Radley bringing up the rear. Everyone present looked expectantly at the rector.

Cassandra cleared her throat. "I know that you have all already been interviewed by Inspector Copper in connection with the death of Professor Tarquin Langley," she began.

"Some of us very recently," came Pandora's acerbic comment.

"But there are still details which he needs to clarify," continued the rector, as if Pandora had not spoken. "And I am therefore grateful on his behalf that you have all been able to attend this evening, in the hope that a resolution can be more swiftly arrived at. So I will hand over to him. Inspector." Cassandra took a seat at the nearest empty table.

Copper stepped forward. "Thank you, Reverend Milton. I hope that I need not detain all of you for longer than necessary." The hint in his words was not lost on all present. "But we may be a little while, and as it looks to me as if Mrs Burley has been busily organising some refreshments, I think it would be a pity to let her efforts go to waste. So sergeant, perhaps you would assist her in serving everyone." Radley, with a surprised look at his superior, stepped forward to take the tray of cups around to the tables, although many refused with a mute shake of the head. "And then perhaps you would like to stand by with your notebook, in case anything emerges which may be worth recording."

As the sergeant completed his circuit and moved to an unobtrusive position out of everyone's eyeline at the rear of the room, attention was focussed once more on the inspector.

"Now as you all know," resumed Copper, "Professor Langley's death was initially presumed to be no more than an unfortunate accident. However, it was soon proved to be more sinister than that, with the revelation that his fall from the museum balcony was occasioned by his having been attacked with one of the museum's exhibits, a piece of masonry. Why would anyone do such a thing? That was one of the first questions that arose. And then we learned that the professor had been sent to the abbey to examine a recently-discovered item in that museum, and that his presence was causing a certain amount of friction."

"A certain amount? I admire your talent for understatement, inspector," remarked Rudolph Wheatley.

Copper gazed at the historian for several long moments, before electing not to rise to the bait. "I needed to find out what reasons there might be for this friction," he continued. "And unfortunately, I'm afraid that not everyone was as candid with me as I might wish. However, I have been lucky enough to have a source of information which might not otherwise have come my way."

Puzzled looks were exchanged between several of those present.

"However, to the point. And my interest was first engaged by the revelation of the identity of the murder weapon. And that directed my attention immediately to the person who apparently discovered it. Mrs Tania Faye."

All eyes turned to Tania.

"So, Mrs Faye," resumed Copper, "I'd like you to account for this discovery of yours." His features took on a stern look, and his voice hardened. "Because a person in my position might very well think that this indicated prior knowledge. And that would make me suspicious." A meaningful look from the inspector indicated to Tania that this was her cue to speak up.

"But, inspector ..." A listener might believe that her tone indicated that she was momentarily flustered by the implied accusation. "I'd never met Professor Langley before. I couldn't possibly have anything against him. Unlike ..." Tania stopped short, as if conscious that she was about to make an uncomfortable disclosure.

"Unlike ... someone else?" jumped in the detective swiftly. "And who might that be, I wonder?"

"I hate to break confidences," said Tania with seeming reluctance, "but I suppose I have no choice."

"In fact, I think I must insist that you do," said Copper. "So please, go on."

"But there's so much hearsay," was Tania's final

ostensible protest.

"I shall have to sort the wheat from the chaff then, shan't I, Mrs Faye?" said Copper. Tania thought she could detect the faintest gleam of humour in his eye. "So please proceed. You said 'unlike'. Unlike whom?"

"Well, I believe that the professor and Mr Wheatley had known each other for many years. And so perhaps there may have been some historical professional rivalry between them."

"Professional rivalry?" erupted Rudolph with a guffaw. "I suppose you might say that. The old fool and I had been sparring partners for years."

"But from what I hear," continued Tania, "it became more than that, once the professor arrived, under orders from the Bishop of Westchester to assess the abbey's recent historical find. The professor was heard to make scathing remarks about both the find and the abbey's museum in which it was hoped to be housed. In fact, more than scathing. He was heard to say that, if he had his way, not only would the manuscript be taken to Westchester, but the museum – a display to which Mr Wheatley had devoted many hours and a great deal of scholarship – would itself be closed down. And Mr Wheatley reacted with some vigour."

"Is this all correct, sir?" demanded the inspector. "Because I think you may have omitted some of those details during your conversations with me about the matter. Did you indeed clash with Professor Langley in those terms? And when Mrs Faye uses the word 'vigour', might she have instead said 'violence'?"

"I don't deny that I was furious with Tarquin over what he was proposing," said Rudolph.

"And you were present in the abbey at the time of the attack on him, sir?"

"I've already said as much, inspector. But that is a far cry from saying that I killed him. Which, I repeat, I did not."

"Perhaps we'll come back to that, Mr Wheatley," said Copper. He turned back to Tania. "Reverting to your use of the word 'unlike', Mrs Faye. I got the impression that you had more than one person in mind when you spoke of a previous acquaintance with the professor."

"I did," said Tania. "Because I became aware that the rector had also known him in the past."

"It's true, I did," spoke up Cassandra. "He was one of the dons during my student years at Camford."

"So, a purely academic relationship?" queried the inspector. "Isn't that how you described it to me? Or has Mrs Faye learned more?"

The rector turned to Tania, a look of appeal in her eye.

"I'm so sorry, Cassandra," said Tania. "But as you said, only the truth will do. In everyone's interests."

"You're right," sighed Cassandra. "You'd better carry on."

"There was a more ... personal aspect to the rector's student relationship with the professor," explained Tania delicately. "Which of course was in no way wrong, in itself, at the time. But under the present circumstances, with the professor and the rector at loggerheads over the fate of the newly-discovered manuscript – I'm afraid that I was told about an extremely hot argument between the two – threats were issued on both sides. Professor Langley threatened to smear the Reverend Milton with unsavoury details of her student life, and the rector retorted with threats against the professor's person."

"Something else which you seem to have unaccountably forgotten to mention during our interviews, rector," remarked Inspector Copper. "And you were also on the abbey's premises when the professor died."

"I was. But I was alone in the vestry, and there was nobody present to corroborate that. I will only offer you two thoughts on the matter. Firstly, that my student years were a long time ago, and time has a habit of giving us the chance to wipe away our follies. And secondly, that I am a firm believer in the validity of the Ten Commandments. Particularly those which say 'Thou shalt not bear false witness', and 'Thou shalt not kill'."

Copper raised his eyebrows. "Well, for the moment, rector, I think I shall take those words at face value, and move on." He craned his neck slightly. "Mrs Clanville. I almost didn't see you behind that pillar. Of course, you're in charge of the abbey's souvenir shop, aren't you? And from what I've seen, very attractive it is. I'm sure that Professor Langley couldn't possibly have had any objection to that. Unless, that is, you happen to know any different, Mrs Faye?" He turned to Tania once again.

"I do know that the professor did have some conversations with Heather," began Tania.

"Me?" burst out Heather. "But I didn't know the man. I'd never seen him before he came here." Gone was the self-assurance of Tania's previous encounter with the shop operator.

"I think we all know that," replied Tania gently. "But the problem was that, when he did come, you took the opportunity to ask his opinion of the organisation of your souvenir shop. A shop which, I think everyone here would agree, is a credit to the abbey, and a valuable addition to its facilities." There was a quiet murmur of agreement, accompanied by gentle nods, around the room. "But sadly, Professor Langley's opinion did not accord with the majority. Very much the reverse, in fact. He was heard expressing derisive judgements on the subject of the project of which you were so very proud. That can't have been anything other than deeply hurtful.

Anyone would have been justifiably upset. And you were seen to visit the professor in the museum in the period prior to his death."

"I just wanted him to know ... I mean, my little shop is loved ... and the children ..." Heather petered out into incoherence.

"But was that all, Mrs Faye?" prompted Copper.

"Unfortunately not," said Tania. "Because after the discovery of the body, Heather was evidently extremely upset. So much so, in fact, that a friend of hers came to collect her and took her across to the Cross Keys for a drink, presumably to steady her nerves. According to the landlord there, Heather was in something of a state. So if I were in your shoes, inspector, I might be asking if that were the natural reaction to the sight of a dead body, or else the result of horrified realisation of the appalling act she had committed."

"We obviously need to consider all possibilities," was the inspector's neutral response, as he studiously ignored the tearful face which Heather turned towards him. "And there are other members of the abbey community who need to be looked at." He appeared to reflect for a moment. "There's the abbey's chief guide, for instance." He regarded Peter. "Mr Hawkley."

"Yes, inspector?"

"Had you known Professor Langley before his arrival here?"

Peter Hawkley shook his head. "Never set eyes on him before, inspector. And, to be frank, I wouldn't mind if I'd never set eyes on him at all."

"Really?" Copper sounded as if his interest was piqued. "I wonder why you say that."

"I don't think the professor was over-impressed with our set-up here," replied Peter.

"I think you may be in danger of understating his opinions, sir," said Copper. "Weren't there some comments passed which were less than glowing?"

"You can't please everyone," shrugged Peter.

"Oh, I gather there may have been more to it than that," remarked the inspector smoothly. "Mrs Faye, weren't you told something of the kind?"

Tania glanced towards Louise Froyle. "Sorry if I'm breaking a confidence, Louise," she said apologetically, "but I think the inspector needs to hear this. You see, inspector, Louise heard the professor making the most disparaging remarks about Peter's manner of carrying out his duties here. And I'm positive that Peter can't have been left unaware of this."

"Not forgetting the fact that Mr Hawkley was of course present around the abbey at the time of the attack."

"Which you already knew, inspector," said Peter. "So were many of the other people here. And when Louise screamed, I rushed up from the crypt to see what had happened."

"He did, inspector," put in Louise. "I saw him coming from that direction."

"So I understand," responded Copper. "Which then brings us to the last member of what I've described as the abbey community we haven't yet considered, and that's Mr Robin Barton. A member of the bell-ringing team, I think."

Robin nodded. "That's correct, inspector."

"And you were also in the abbey on the evening in question, weren't you, sir?"

"I was," confirmed Robin. "For a rehearsal. Which was over long before the professor's death."

"This is all ridiculous," intervened Tom hotly. "Rob had never met Professor Langley before he came to Ramston. He'd probably never even heard of him. So what on earth could he have to gain by killing him?"

The detective gave a small grim smile. "Certainly

nothing that has emerged on the occasions that he and I have spoken. But perhaps Mrs Faye has better information than I do." He raised an eyebrow in Tania's direction.

"If Inspector Copper were in possession of all the facts," said Tania, "he might think that the thing Robin had to gain was peace of mind." The people scattered around the room gave Tania a variety of quizzical looks. "You see," she continued, "the professor ... it's very difficult to know how to put this ... he had made a certain suggestion to Robin, based on what he believed he knew about him. A very unsavoury suggestion, which was overheard by ... one of those present here." Tania studiously avoided looking in Louise's direction. "And there was a threat of unpleasant consequences to Robin's reputation if he refused to comply. Which, by the look of his reaction which was witnessed by someone else, he did refuse. Isn't that the general gist of what happened, Robin?"

Robin took a deep gulp of air. "All right, yes. But," he said, his voice gaining strength, "everyone who knows me knows who I am."

"And nobody who knows Rob would believe a word of whatever filth Langley was threatening to spread," declared Tom. "Besides, he wasn't even in the abbey when the professor met his death. His bell-ringing rehearsal was long over. And in fact, he was home with me. And I'd be prepared to swear to that in court, inspector." He glared defiantly at Copper.

The inspector permitted himself a quiet smile. "I don't think there will be any need for you to go as far as perjuring yourself, sir," he replied. "Because although Mr Barton apparently can't account for his time with the corroboration of any witnesses, there is also no witness to state that he returned to the abbey after his initial departure. Or second departure, I should say. But still well before the professor met his end."

"I went to the park," said Robin. "I just wanted to be alone. I was shaking. But there was nobody else around, so I can't prove it. But I heard the abbey clock strike half-past nine, and I suddenly realised that Tom would be home wondering where I was. So I left." He visibly slumped in his chair, as Tom put a protective arm around his shoulders.

"Which then brings me," continued Copper, "to the last of those here who was involved with Professor Langley on the evening of his death. The other person not part of the abbey community, who had also apparently left the premises before the professor's death."

"Don't pussy-foot, inspector," responded Pandora Weston. "You're plainly referring to me. Although I quarrel with your use of the term 'involved with' when speaking of the situation between Langley and myself."

"My apologies, Miss Weston," said the inspector. "Of course, I realise that you would always prefer to choose your words carefully, being an author. Which, as I understand it, was the reason why there arose a contretemps between you and the professor. Because there was something of a confrontation, wasn't there?"

"We certainly had words," admitted the author.

"About your books?"

"Everyone's a critic," said Pandora, attempting a light laugh. "One can't expect glowing reviews all the time."

"Oh, I believe it was more than that," said Copper. "In fact, I'm led to believe that there are two witnesses to the seriousness of the argument between you. Wasn't there some sort of public spat in the Cross Keys restaurant? Perhaps somebody could remind me of the landlord's name. Mrs Faye, can you help me out?"

"Oh yes, inspector," said Tania. "In fact, Dennis Dean happened to mention to me that there had been very hot words passing between the professor and Miss Weston. Oh ... and I've just remembered something else." She paused artistically.

"Do go on, Mrs Faye," said Copper, an amused glint in his eye. He was obviously enjoying the performance. "If you have something else helpful to contribute."

"People do chat to me, inspector," murmured Tania apologetically. "And I think someone mentioned that they'd heard the professor speaking of 'plagiarism' when referring to Pandora's books. That was back in the abbey, later on. Of course, the very idea would be ridiculous. Pandora is such a very popular author amongst the readers at my library, and having read all her novels, I can vouch for the originality of all her work."

"Well, thank you for that, Tania," said Pandora drily. "I'm very glad to be so generously vindicated."

"But even so," remarked Copper, "I can understand that the merest suggestion of plagiarism could be extremely damaging to an author's reputation, however well-thought-of she might be. Didn't Shakespeare have a line about 'He who filches from me my good name', or something of the sort? I remember my former guv'nor quoting it to me in one of our old cases. Mud sticks. And to disprove such a charge would be very difficult. A person might well go to extreme lengths to avoid such a situation. They might well confront their accuser, with drastic results."

"They might well, inspector," responded Pandora, her head held high. "Perhaps I might decide to use such a plot line in one of my future novels. But of course, your problem would be that I was nowhere near the abbey when the professor's death occurred. If there is a witness to our contretemps, as you describe it, then they will know that it occurred much earlier in the evening. After which I left the abbey, and did not return. I know I can't prove that I didn't. But equally, you can't prove that I did!"

Chapter 20
Tuesday

"As you can see," observed Inspector Copper, "I have a fine set of motives to consider. Motives which, ladies and gentlemen, you have been reluctant to reveal to me, understandably, I suppose. Nobody would wish to put themselves in the frame unnecessarily when there is a charge of murder in prospect. So my thanks go to Mrs Faye for her help in bringing all this information to my attention, even though you may not all agree with the sentiment. My other main consideration, of course, is the question of opportunity to commit the crime. Who was placed where, and when? And can we narrow down the time of the attack?"

"Do you know, inspector, I think we may be able to," interposed Rudolph Wheatley. "Because, now I come to think about it, I heard some sort of a thud from where I was sitting in the side chapel, and I thought 'I ought to make a move, because that must be Peter locking up', but I looked at my watch and realised it wasn't quite twenty-five past nine. And then I also realised that it wasn't the usual loud crash that the Jerusalem Porch door makes when you close it. It was much more muted. But I didn't think any more of it, and then it was driven from my mind when Louise screamed. But, on reflection, it must have been the sound of the professor hitting the ground."

"He's right!" suddenly said Heather Clanville. "I heard it too. I was in my shop, and I heard the same thing, except that I thought it was someone coming in through the exit door by my shop and slamming it behind them. But I looked, and there was nobody there, so it couldn't have been. If somebody had come in, I would have been bound to see them. And that was just a few minutes before we all heard Louise, so it must have been the same thing that Mr Wheatley heard."

"That's very helpful information," said Copper. "Perhaps it might have been even more helpful if it had been volunteered earlier on," he remarked drily, "but we are where we are. So I'll move on. Let me, for the sake of argument, take at face value Mr Barton's statement that he left the park at half-past nine, when he heard the abbey clock strike. If he was in the park at that time, he couldn't have been in the abbey five minutes earlier, attacking the professor, because if he had been, he would have had to make a remarkably swift exit, and I find it highly unlikely that he could have done so unobserved. There were people about, and once more, the door to the Jerusalem Porch is proving to be an excellent mute – well, perhaps not so mute – witness. To leave the abbey by that route could not have been unnoticed. And if he had hidden and left later, he couldn't have got home at the time he did. And in this instance, I will not quarrel with Mr Headley's testimony. So I am prepared to accept Mr Barton's account of his movements."

"Oh, inspector," intervened Pandora Weston. A cat-like smile spread across her features. "I have just realised that you are going to have to accept my account of my movements as well."

"And why do I have to do so, Miss Weston?" queried Copper.

"Because I too," smirked Pandora, "have a witness. Like the Jerusalem Porch door, it's a mute witness, but I think you'll find its testimony compelling."

"I'm afraid I have no idea what you're referring to, Miss Weston," responded the puzzled detective. "Could you please explain who or what you mean?"

"My laptop," said Pandora. "When I arrived home after my little spat with Professor Langley, I was still absolutely seething, but at the same time, I had all sorts of thoughts whirling around in my brain about a plot for a new novel. It would be a Sister Catherine mystery, and it would centre around the sort of discovery that had been made at the abbey. So before I could forget all the ideas that were jostling about in my mind, I decided to make notes of them in a new file on my computer, so I turned it on and sat at it for a while."

"I'm not certain where this is leading, Miss Weston, unless you had somebody else there to see you do all this."

"But don't you see? The computer is my witness. Now I may not be a technical wizard, but even I know that computers keep some sort of log of their activity – when they're turned on, what time such-and-such a file is saved, and so on. And I always save as I go, so there'll be lots of time checks. Now, inspector, I'm perfectly happy for you to let your technical people take a look at my laptop, and they will see the time I turned it on, and the period of activity that took place, which I'm sure will easily cover the period the professor was attacked. Will that do you?" Pandora sat back and folded her arms in triumph.

Copper's eyebrows rose in surprise. "Well, Miss Weston, that's all very well argued. In fact," he added with a smile, "I shouldn't be at all astonished if you were to use that alibi device in some future murder mystery. Not Sister Cat, obviously. And should it prove necessary, I shall certainly take you up on your offer to inspect your computer." His smile faded. "But I think that such action may not be necessary. Because I believe we are coming much closer to discovering the truth about Professor Langley's death. There are just two more people whose accounts I would like to verify – Mr Hawkley, and the Reverend Milton. One of whom was visible about the abbey at various times – one of whom was not."

"I assume that last observation was directed at me, inspector," said Cassandra Milton. "And you're right. I don't have anyone to account for my movements at the crucial time, for the simple reason that I was ensconced in my vestry, occupied with paperwork concerning the administration of the abbey. Not glamorous work, I grant you, but it needs to be done, and usually alone. And, sadly, not with benefit of computer."

"And I imagine that you must have been filled with thoughts concerning the administration of the abbey, rector, in the wake of your conversations with the professor," said Copper. "Especially the last one in the museum, less than an hour before his death. There would have been your personal situation to consider – how would you have been placed if the threatened revelations concerning your past had been made public? Then there was the position of the abbey in relation to your ecclesiastical superior. If your bishop had made decisions with which you violently disagreed, would you have been prepared to defy him? What hold did Professor Langley have over you, and how could it be countered? That would all have given you a great deal to think about."

"And think about it I did," retorted the rector vehemently. "But that's all I did. And the only thing that interrupted my thoughts was the sound of a scream coming from my church. A scream which I hurried to investigate. As you have been told. And there were several people who were witnesses to me doing so."

"Including Mr Hawkley, I believe."

"Exactly," said Cassandra.

"That's right, inspector," broke in Peter. "The rector rushed past me to get to whatever was going on."

"No, that's not right," said Heather, frowning. "It was the other way round. You were the one who pushed past the rector and me. And I remember thinking of the old saying about not being in too much of a hurry to meet bad news half-way."

"Well, whichever it was," shrugged Peter. "I dare say we were all confused. But you saw me come up from the crypt, didn't you, rector? Because I'm sure I was ahead of you then."

Cassandra shook her head, puzzled. "Actually, I don't remember that," she said. "I mean, I know you were there somewhere."

"Well, somebody must have seen me," insisted Peter, looking round in appeal.

Adrian Hinton cleared his throat. "The only thing I remember is seeing Peter up in the museum somewhere around that time, but that must have been before. And that's the whole length of the church away from the crypt. I mean, nobody can be in two places at once, can they?"

"Indeed not," said the inspector. "For instance, you, Mr Hawkley, can't have been both behind and ahead of the rector in your move towards the site of Professor Langley's body. So which was it?"

"I ... um ... I ..." floundered Peter.

"And why would you be so insistent that you appeared from the crypt, rather than from any other direction?" persisted Copper.

"But he did come from there," repeated Louise. "I've told you, I saw him. So how could he have been up in the museum? It doesn't make sense."

"I'm afraid that it does," said Copper heavily. "And I'm once again indebted to Mrs Faye for telling me how."

Tania let out a deep sigh. "Oh Peter," she said. She gave a sad smile. "You're so proud of the abbey and what you do for it. And you were so happy to tell us about the parties of schoolchildren you take around, passing on your love for the place, and how you always finish your tour with a visit to the crypt and then a trip along what you tell them is the 'secret passage'. And it almost is, isn't it? Probably not many people realise that it's there, running from the base of the bell tower, underneath the nave, through to the crypt. Providing a quick way to get from one to the other without being seen by anyone else in the abbey. That's how you got to the crypt at the crucial time. And that's why you were so desperate to prove that you were at the far end of the church, well away from the museum, when the professor was killed."

In the deep silence that followed, all eyes were fixed on Peter Hawkley, frozen into stillness as he was, as expressions ranging from perplexity to disbelief could be seen on the faces of everyone present.

Eventually, Inspector Copper spoke up. "Mr Hawkley," he said gently, "do you have anything to say?"

Peter gave a helpless shrug. "What can I say, inspector? Tania is right, of course. I was responsible for Professor Langley's death. And I wish I could say how sorry I am to have brought all this grief and distress upon you all, but ..." His voice faded out.

"Perhaps you'd just like to tell us exactly what happened, sir," prompted Copper.

Sergeant Radley moved to stand at the guide's shoulder, his notebook poised. "Sir," he murmured to his superior, "before the gentleman speaks, shouldn't you ...?"

"Caution me?" Peter's face wore a faint sad smile. "Perhaps it's a little late for that, sergeant. You all heard what I said. But carry on, if you must. Or shall we consider it done?" He looked up at the inspector.

Copper hesitated. He seemed to be in two minds. "If you wish, sir."

"It wasn't planned." A strange calm seemed to have settled over Peter. "But I can't say it wasn't deserved." His brow creased in puzzlement. "Why did he have to be like that with everybody?" He stopped, gazing unfocussed into some unseen distance.

"Peter," urged Cassandra Milton softly, "I think we all need to know what happened. For our own peace of mind, if nothing else."

"It was almost time for me to close up the abbey to visitors," began Peter. "I was just going on my rounds, as usual, and as part of that, I went up to the museum. And I was surprised that Professor Langley was still there. For some reason, I thought he'd already gone. But what surprised me more was that he was poring over the new Book of Hours with some sort of gleam in his eye. He looked as if he was actually gloating. And I asked if I could help him at all. He just laughed at me. He said he didn't need my help – he was going to help himself. And I asked what he meant, and he said that the Book of Hours was far too precious an object to leave in the possession of a bunch of ignorant provincials, so he was going to make sure that it was kept in proper conditions by people who understood its true worth. So then I asked if it was true – that the manuscript was genuine, as we all hoped. 'Genuine?' he said, with a sneer. 'It's the finest thing I've ever held in my hands. It's a gem." So I said that the rector and everybody else would be delighted, because it would enhance the abbey's reputation no end. And he said 'Reputation? What reputation? I hope you aren't referring to those pathetic little guided tours you give. They're never going to impress anyone who knows anything. And as for the rector, I wonder if her own reputation isn't going to need a great deal of enhancing if she doesn't play ball with me. Surrounded as she is by a crew of inadequates. Henry VIII had the right idea' he said. 'Strip the whole place of hangers-on and frivolous nonsense, starting with this excuse for a museum'."

The rector shook her head in disbelief. "I never imagined for a moment that the Tarquin Langley I knew could have turned into this ..." Words seemed to fail her.

"Monster?" said Peter. "He was, rector. You shouldn't grieve for him. He didn't just want the book. He wanted to take everything we loved away from us. He'd have stopped me from coming here to work. And my wife

..." His voice broke.

"Wife?" mouthed the puzzled inspector to Cassandra.

"Peter's late wife lies here in our precinct," she explained.

"I come here every day to be near her," resumed Peter tearfully. "And if I'd been kept away because of that man, I don't know what I would have done."

"Oh Peter," said Cassandra with a sigh, "you should know I'd never have prevented you ... " she tailed off, lost for words.

"But my museum?" Rudolph Wheatley sounded stunned and hurt. "After all the effort that so many people have put into that ..."

"Oh, he didn't care about that," said Peter. "He just looked around and laughed. He called the exhibits a mishmash of rubbish and irrelevancies. 'I mean,' he said, 'look at this,' and he picked up the Earl of Wessex's boss. 'This for a star exhibit? I ask you. Who's ever going to be excited by a sad lump of painted stone?' And he just threw it down in contempt. He picked up the Book of Hours and turned away to look at it. 'But this ...' Gloating, he was. And I picked up the boss and ... well, before I knew it, I had gone up behind him and smashed it over the back of his head. I must have been so enraged. And he was standing by the parapet, and he pitched straight over and landed on the floor below. And I just stood there frozen for a moment. I was horrified at what I'd done, and my only thought was to get as far away as possible, so I put the boss back and then ran down the stairs to the lowest level so that I could go along the bottom passage to the crypt. Maybe I had some idea of hiding myself away. But then I heard Louise scream, and the sound of people running, so I came back up and ..."

"... and we know what happened next," said Copper. He gave a deep exhalation and faced the room.

"Ladies and gentlemen, I think we needn't detain the rest of you any longer. If you wish to leave, you are at liberty to do so, but we may be in touch with you again if we require any further statements. In the meantime ... Mr Hawkley ... we have to go. Sergeant, if you would, please."

Sergeant Radley placed a hand under Peter's elbow to assist him to his feet, and the small procession of three made its way out of the Holy Grail into the main body of the abbey.

Cassandra Milton stood. "Ladies and gentlemen," she announced in calm muted tones. "I shall be offering prayers at the high altar in just a few moments. If anyone wishes to join me ..." She followed in the footsteps of the police, leaving the others in the Holy Grail exchanging mute looks of amazement and speculation.

*

"Jenny, what on earth brings you here?" enquired a surprised Tania as she manoeuvred the library's returns cart between rows of shelving.

"I sneaked out," explained the breathless dental nurse. "We had a cancellation, so I had a few moments free to come across from the surgery. But is it true what they're saying? Have they caught the person who murdered that professor at the abbey?"

"Yes," replied Tania. "The police made an arrest last night."

"And was it you who solved the case for them?" demanded Jenny excitedly. "I bet it was."

"In the end, there was a confession." Tania was reluctant to volunteer too much information.

"Oh, come on. You can't get away with that. I want to hear about the whole thing. In detail."

"Oh, very well," conceded Tania. "Otherwise I suppose I shall never hear the end of it. But not here, and not now. And you'd better get back to the surgery double quick, or else you'll end up getting murdered yourself."

"Me?" Jenny laughed uproariously, shattering the peace of the library. "Who'd ever want to murder me?"

*　　*　　*

also by Roger Keevil

The Inspector Constable Murder Mysteries

Murderer's Fête
Who could have foreseen the murder of a clairvoyant at a country fête?

Murder Unearthed
Sun, sangria and suspects during a supposed holiday in Spain

Death Sails In The Sunset
Murder ensues when a journalist won't let guilty secrets be buried at sea

Murder Comes To Call
Three short stories to tax the talents of our detectives

Murder Most Frequent
Another trilogy of intriguing cases for Constable and Copper

The Odds On Murder
Who is riding for a fall when a prominent racehorse trainer is killed?

No Bar To Murder
Complicated relationships make a potent and lethal cocktail

The Murder Cabinet
A return to Dammett Hall leaves the nation's fate in the team's hands

The Game Of Murder
Sudden death at the TV studio as entertainment turns to murder;
PLUS a bonus short story, 'Exit A Murderer',
and a full index to all the Inspector Constable mysteries

The Copper & Co Murder Mysteries

Murderer's Honeymoon
Even on an idyllic tropical island, murder never takes a holiday

Murder At Witch's Holt
Dark secrets lead to a strange death at a spooky manor house

Buccaneer's Murder
A wealthy businessman lies dead aboard his luxury private yacht

The Ramston Murder Mysteries

Murdered By Moonlight
Dramatic death at a Cornish open-air theatre

* * *

Printed in Great Britain
by Amazon